A SORE LOSER

"Mr. Reggoner and I have some business, sir." Dex graced the redhead with his very best smile—when he really worked at it he could smile a smile that would warm a matron's heart—and bowed. "I apologize for the intrusion, miss, particularly so since we haven't yet been introduced."

"I owe you nothing, damn you," Reggoner butted in.

Dex hadn't paid all that much attention to Reggoner before. Now he did so. And did not overmuch care for what he saw. He was clean shaven and wore a silk hat and cravat—a rather tastelessly gaudy one—and lacquered pumps under spotless spats. A fop, no doubt, he decided critically. Probably carried a lace hanky in his sleeve, too. Dex sniffed in disdain.

"The wager, sir, was _____ ___ winnings, sir, are now mi___ _____ er or be damned. ___

Reggo___ _____ to full height. "I_ _____ __n and a cheat. An_ _____

"If I we__ __ _____man, sir, you would now be flat on your ass." Dex remembered himself in time to give the young lady a smile. "My apologies, miss."

He was looking at the redhead and very nearly missed seeing the fist that came whistling in the direction of his jaw . . .

DON'T MISS THESE
ALL-ACTION WESTERN SERIES
FROM THE BERKLEY PUBLISHING GROUP

THE GUNSMITH by J. R. Roberts
    Clint Adams was a legend among lawmen, outlaws, and ladies.
    They called him . . . the Gunsmith.

LONGARM by Tabor Evans
    The popular long-running series about U.S. Deputy Marshal
    Long—his life, his loves, his fight for justice.

SLOCUM by Jake Logan
    Today's longest-running action Western. John Slocum rides
    a deadly trail of hot blood and cold steel.

BUSHWHACKERS by B. J. Lanagan
    An action-packed series by the creators of Longarm! The
    rousing adventures of the most brutal gang of cutthroats
    ever assembled—Quantrill's Raiders.

DIAMONDBACK

TEXAS TWO-TIMING

Guy Brewer

JOVE BOOKS, NEW YORK

This is a work of fiction. Names, characters, places, and incidents are
either the product of the author's imagination or are used fictitiously,
and any resemblance to actual persons, living or dead, business
establishments, events or locales is entirely coincidental.

TEXAS TWO-TIMING

A Jove Book / published by arrangement with
the author

PRINTING HISTORY
Jove edition / November 1999

All rights reserved.
Copyright © 1999 by Penguin Putnam Inc.
This book may not be reproduced in whole or in part,
by mimeograph or any other means, without permission.
For information address: The Berkley Publishing Group,
a division of Penguin Putnam Inc.,
375 Hudson Street, New York, New York 10014.

The Penguin Putnam Inc. World Wide Web site address is
http://www.penguinputnam.com

ISBN: 0-515-12685-3

A JOVE BOOK®
Jove Books are published by The Berkley Publishing Group,
a division of Penguin Putnam Inc.,
375 Hudson Street, New York, New York 10014.
JOVE and the "J" design
are trademarks belonging to Penguin Putnam Inc.

PRINTED IN THE UNITED STATES OF AMERICA

10 9 8 7 6 5 4 3 2 1

◆ 1 ◆

He tasted the wine. It was a dark ruby red in color and very sweet to the taste. Definitely a dessert wine appropriate for serving with fruit and cheese. Well, this was dessert he was having now. Sort of.

Dex smiled, dipped the tip of his forefinger into the wine and transferred a bold drop of the liquid onto Helena's left nipple.

"Oooo! That's cold."

Smiling, Dex allowed his tongue to follow where the finger had been.

"Oh. That's nice."

He suckled gently at the small, elongated, raisin-like protuberance of rubbery flesh, and Helena sighed and began to wriggle.

She rolled to the side, taking that nipple away from him and offering the other. Dex obliged by giving that one his attention as well.

"You do know how to make a girl feel good, sir."

"Dex," he reminded her. "Dexter Yancey." He smiled and lightly kissed the tender flat that lay between her breasts. "At your service, my dear."

"You're sweet."

"And you are pretty. I would say that makes for a most rewarding combination, would you not agree?"

"You ain't from around here are you, honey?"

"No," Dex admitted. "Indeed I ain't."

Helena giggled. "You sound funny when you say that. I mean . . . I'm not trying to poke fun at you nasty-like. Nothing like that. But when I say 'ain't' it comes out just natural. You know? But when you say it, it don't." Her pretty face, surrounded by a wreath of shiny black curls, screwed into a frown. "Am I making sense t'you, honey?"

"You make a great deal of sense to me, dear girl. Now if you would be so good as to lie flat for a moment . . . ah, that is ever so much better, thank you."

Helena giggled again and reached down to guide Dex's entry as he rolled over the nearer of her legs and positioned himself above her. "Ooo!"

"I agree," he said.

"That's . . . nice."

"Mm hmm."

"And that's even nicer." She sounded pleased. Her hips began to rise and fall in time with Dex's movements, the girl meeting his slow and gentle thrusts.

She was a lovely little thing, no more than twenty if she was that old, with a slim body, ample hips and shapely legs. Her breasts were more than the proverbial mouthful. More, indeed, than a hearty handful. And she had a face that would have been entirely appropriate if depicted on a cameo brooch.

Dex ignored the ages-old admonition against it and kissed her, his tongue exploring the inside of her mouth while a significant other portion of his anatomy continued its explorations elsewhere.

Helena's eyes grew wide and she gasped. She stared at him. And after a moment began to cry.

Dex stopped in mid stroke and withdrew from the moist and pleasant warmth of the girl's body. "What's wrong? Did I hurt you?"

"You . . . you kissed me."

"Yes. Is there something wrong with that?"

"Nobody . . . nobody ever kissed me before."

"Nobody?"

"Well not . . . that is . . . there was a kid. Billy, his name was. We was just little. Nine, ten, like that. He kissed me once. Sort of. He made me squeeze my eyes real tight closed and then he kinda pecked me in the face real quick and then he ran away. I pretended I didn't know what he was gonna do but I really did."

"And that was your only . . . ?" He used the ball of his thumb to wipe the tears from her eyes and lightly kissed each spot as if to blot them away. He could taste the salt on his lips.

She shrugged. "I understand. Honest I do. Gentlemen don't kiss whores. That's just the way it is."

Dex kissed her again. "I don't think of you as a whore."

She laughed to make sure he knew she was joking, then said, "If you think you're gonna get by with not paying me for my time t'night . . ."

Dex laughed too and kissed first her forehead, then each of her eyes again and finally her mouth. Deeply and long.

"You really are awful sweet, honey. I mean, Dex. See? I haven't forgot. Would you . . . would you mind if I was t'kiss you back?"

"I'd like that," he said.

Helena sighed and hugged him with a fierce, sudden strength. And then, her mood quite gay, she pulled his head down and set about experimenting with the art and science of the kiss.

The remainder of the evening, Dex would've had to admit, became better and better still from that point onward.

· 2 ·

"Damn, you're a noisy son of a bitch," James complained as he blinked and yawned and reluctantly woke to the clatter of Dexter's boots hitting the floor. "What time is it anyhow?"

Dex grinned. "A little past sun-up. Time for lazy bastards like you to be up and about, don't you think?"

"What I think is that you could have had the decency to be quiet when you finished your tomcatting around."

"Kind of like you were a couple mornings back?"

"That was different. Besides, my girl was pretty. Yours . . ." James made a face. "She wouldn't have been so bad if she had a little color to her. But that pale, pasty skin . . . ugh. I don't see how you can stand it."

Dex laughed. James himself was no victim of pale and pasty flesh tones. Not hardly. James was Dex's best friend and traveling companion; there was a time, back before the war, when James had also been Dexter's personal property. When they were children Dex was the son of a Louisiana planter, and James was a slave, the child of the Yancey family's cook and an unknown father. James had been given to Dex as a playmate. That status had not lasted past emancipation but their friendship had endured, although they took care to hide that fact most of the time unless they were alone.

"Thinking of looks," James added, "you look like Hell warmed over."

Dex glanced in the mirror that hung on the wall of their Benson, Texas, hotel room. The fact was, James was unfortunately right about that. He did look like hell. Bags under his eyes. Beard stubble. Bloodred veins shining like lanterns around the usual brown of his eyes. Yeah, he looked like hell all right.

"You should be so lucky as to look like me, black boy," Dex shot back.

In point of fact, James did look quite a lot like Dexter. At twenty-eight, Dex was a lean and fit five foot eleven in height with dark blond hair, Burnside whiskers flowing onto the shelf of a finely chiseled jaw and features that more than a handful of the ladies seemed to find attractive indeed.

James was a year younger and half an inch taller. A straight nose and thin lips bespoke a heavy infusion of white blood in his background, although his mother was as dark as coal. James's skin tone was that of a superior grade of milk chocolate. Apart from that, though, he and Dex might have been mistaken for kin.

"What I should be so lucky," James said, "is to be able to get some damn sleep. Can't you hush and let a body rest?"

"Getting lazy, are you?"

"No, tired. You aren't the only one who stayed up late last night."

"Excuse me. I didn't know."

"Of course you didn't. Us darkies don't let you white boys know anything more than we have to, y'know."

"Ah, I see. Now I understand everything."

"Good, but can you do it quietly, please?"

"I'll shut up on one condition. Tell me what you did with the razor."

"It's in the top drawer of the nightstand," James said. "You want me to go down and fetch your hot water?"

"I can do it, thanks."

"Those folks downstairs will think it's funny you getting your own water when you got a servant to do for you."

"Hey, us white boys don't tell everything we know either. Now be quiet, will you? You're keeping yourself awake." Dex chuckled and left the room in search of hot water to shave with.

James rolled over to place his back to the door and closed his eyes. Last night had been long and more than a little tiring. He was already snoring by the time Dex returned with a pitcher of steaming water.

• 3 •

Breakfast was one of Dexter's favorite meals, and whenever possible he liked to spend an appropriate amount of time in the selection and enjoyment of the day's initial meal. The scents that greeted him as he entered the dining room of the Planters Rest made his mouth water in anticipation of what was to come.

He was greeted at the doorway by an obsequious black man old enough to be Dex's father who bowed low and led Dexter to a table beside the front windows. James followed close behind Dexter, playing the public role of the faithful and biddable manservant.

The aging waiter handed Dex a menu with a flourish and nodded toward James, who had taken up position half a pace behind his old friend. "You want your man fed this mornin', suh?"

"I do, uncle."

"We got a place in the back for he to eat, suh."

"That will be fine, thank you." Dex swiveled in his chair to speak to James. "I won't be needing you until later, James. You can go with this man for now."

"Yes, sir, thank you, sir." A spark of amusement glinted

in James's eyes as he mouthed the necessary words and bowed as if in deep appreciation.

Dex waved airily in dismissal. "Go on now. And when you come back, uncle, bring me a pot of tea to start with. China Black if you have it. I'll decide on my meal in the meantime."

"Yes, suh, as you say, suh." The waiter bowed and backed away two steps before he turned and beckoned James to follow him out through a door that would presumably lead to the kitchen and the working sections of the hotel building.

Dex took up a snowy white linen napkin and shook it out, only mildly annoyed that the service of placing the napkin into his lap hadn't been performed for him by the waiter.

"Good morning, sir."

"I beg your pardon?" Dex said, turning to see who was speaking. It was one of three men seated at a nearby table, all of them dressed in business suits and boiled shirts with celluloid collars. "Are we acquainted, sir?" he asked, knowing perfectly well that they were not.

"Forgive me for intrudin', sir, but I couldn't help but notice your arrival. Noticed too that you seem a gentleman of the . . . shall we say . . . old school. There was a man—I won't call him a gentleman—came through here a few months back. Surveyor, he was. Had some niggers with him on his chain crew. Wanted those niggers to eat right here in the dining room alongside of white folks. Can you believe it, sir? It's shameful the way things have gotten."

Dex clucked and tut-tutted sympathetically and shook his head with a display of great sadness. "Shameful," he murmured.

The fellow at the other table stood, forgetting the napkin that was spread over his lap. The napkin slithered onto the floor unnoticed. "May I introduce myself, sir? I am B. Tyler Whitcomb of the North Carolina Whitcombs. My companions are Grady Moore and Alexander Peacock."

First Whitcomb and then each of the other gentlemen in turn rose—Moore and Peacock did, however, remember to take their napkins off their laps before standing—and shook Dex's hand.

"I'm Dexter Lee Yancey of the Louisiana Yanceys."

"Of course, sir. I am familiar with the name," Whitcomb said. Dex rather seriously doubted that Whitcomb had ever heard of the Yancey clan. Very few outside northern Louisiana would have. Still, it was a polite thing to say and not the sort of fib Dex would hold against a man.

"Proud to make your acquaintance, sir," Dex responded, "and yours gentlemen."

"We are just finishing our meal, Mr. Yancey, or we would be pleased to have you join us." It was an invitation that was entirely genuine, Dex was sure.

"Another time, sir," Dex said.

"By all means." Whitcomb glanced back at his breakfast companions for a moment, then turned his attention again to the stranger in their midst. "Tell me, sir. Are you a sporting man?"

"I have no facility with cards, if that is what you mean." For a moment Dexter wondered if his instincts had failed him, wondered if these "gentlemen" were adventurers in search of a pigeon to pluck.

"Actually, Mr. Yancey, my thoughts lay more along the line of equestrian pursuits."

"Riding to the hounds, sir?" Dex asked. It was not something he'd heard was common in Texas. In Virginia, yes, or Maryland, but . . . Even so, Dex knew very little about Texas. Perhaps they did . . .

Whitcomb laughed. "Not after fox tails, Mr. Yancey. Racing is our passion hereabouts. Flat racing. And . . . may I offer a confession, Mr. Yancey?"

"Please."

"I own the bank here. I happened to be looking out my office window several days ago when you and your nigger rode in. My bank is immediately across the street from the hotel, you see. And I happened to take note of that rather nice looking animal of yours. Very handsome. He looks quite fast. It occurred to me, well, if he runs as nicely as he looks . . ." Whitcomb smiled and spread his hands.

"Ah, now that is something else entirely," Dex agreed.

"Would you be interested in a sporting proposition, Mr. Yancey?"

"I could well be tempted, Mr. Whitcomb," Dex admitted.

"We have an organization of sorts, Mr. Yancey. A gentleman's club, one might say. We hold meets on alternating Saturdays."

"And this Saturday coming . . . ?" Dex suggested.

"By happy coincidence, Mr. Yancey, we will indeed be racing on Saturday next."

"We'd be right pleased to have you there as our guest, Yancey," one of the others put in. Peacock, Dex thought that one was. Yes, of course. Peacock had a faint hint of red in his hair and fuller cheeks than the other one, whose name was—it took Dex a moment to recall it—Moore, that was it. Alex Peacock and something Moore. Grady. Grady Moore. He made a mental note to keep them straight.

That was only the polite thing to do since the gentlemen were obliging enough to offer a contribution to Dex and James's wallets.

Because if it was a horse race they had in mind, well, victory was as certain as sunrise. Dex had no doubts about that whatsoever.

He managed somehow to contain his glee and to offer polite good-byes when the local gentlemen excused themselves to go about their affairs.

And on top of that stroke of fine fortune, the Planters Rest hotel did indeed stock China Black tea.

Dex considered this a day most wonderfully launched.

• 4 •

"You're telling me that *they* came to *you*?" James doubled over with laughter. "You didn't have to talk them into it?"

Dex grinned. "I'm telling you the truth. They're the ones who suggested it. I would have found a way eventually, of course. But I didn't have to. The gents took one look at me . . . had taken a look already to the horse . . . and rose to the bait like a trout to a mayfly."

James's laughter got all the louder. "Lordy, we must be living right."

"Hold it down, will you? They can probably hear you all through the hotel."

"I got to stop anyhow," James wheezed. "My belly hurts." He did manage to put a stop to the noise, but he couldn't quit grinning. "Admire that magnificent horse of yours, do they?"

Dex was grinning rather broadly himself. "I told you that animal was gonna come in mighty handy."

The horse in question was an exceptionally fine-looking bay gelding, a leggy animal with a thin neck and finely shaped head if a trifle narrow in the chest and forequarters.

It had a lean and sinuous profile and the fluid gait of a cat. The horse just plain looked fast.

Looked. That was the important word in that particular regard. And looks may oft deceive.

The horse, which they'd renamed Galahad, did not live up to its appearance, poor thing. As James put it after giving the horse a try-out, Galahad would very likely come in second to his own shadow . . . even if he was running toward a setting sun.

It did, however, have one redeeming ability. That was the reason Dex had insisted that he and James possess Galahad regardless of cost.

Fortunately the previous owner, a gentleman back in Shreveport, had proven more than eager to unload the seven-year-old bay, he apparently having placed his faith in Galahad's appearance and lost a considerable amount of hard cash in consequence.

Dex had come into knowledge of Galahad when he tried to inveigle the Shreveport gentleman into a wee wager and was immediately afterward subjected to a torrent of complaint. Including, quite significantly, mention of certain tricks taught to the handsome slug by its original owner, who seemed to have been a young woman of soft demeanor but little principle.

"Damn her," the Shreveport man had complained. "She took me. Oh, she took me. I admit to it. She knew what she was doing, and that's the fact of it. Couldn't run the horse to demonstrate his speed, she said. But I could see for myself what a fine, sound animal he was. Well, I saw, all right. Believed her lies, damn her. Paid . . . never mind what I paid for this beast, young man. I'd be ashamed to tell you. More ashamed to sell him to you under false pretenses. I won't consider selling this son of a bitch unless you know the truth about him. No sir, I won't. But . . . you say you might want him anyway? Aye, I would most certainly be interested in making a trade with you. Your mare looks sound. I can see she has solid breeding behind her, sir. You, uh, how much boot would you ask if we were to think about the swap, eh? I wouldn't give you full value for the mare. I tell you that straight out. I would want a little off the price for this bay. Not that he's worth a tinker's damn, no sir, but I won't trade him off without getting at least a little something back of what I paid in order to arrange my own fleecing. If that does not offend you though, sir, why, let's go inside the tavern there and see if we can come to some, um, accommodation, shall we?''

That had been a little over a week ago.

And now, bless their hearts, it looked like a trio of gentlemen in Benson, Texas, would be the proof of Dex's wisdom in swapping for good old bog-slow Galahad.

Yes sir, he thought, there were times when life looked rather good indeed, and this morning was very much one of them.

◆ 5 ◆

Dex left the hotel and went around to the back of the tall building to the low-roofed shed where guests were allowed to stable their horses if they'd arrived by means of their own transportation.

Dex and James chose to use the hotel stable rather than the distant Benson livery not to save the half dollar or so it would have cost for livery care but in order to keep close to them their most valued possession, for the animal that was standing there was the foundation upon which rested the financial well-being of them both.

Both men ignored the handsome bay gelding that had prompted the local gents to offer a wager and went instead to the stall of a tall, pale yellow animal with ears like semaphore flags and a ratty little scrap of tail that would have embarrassed a chipmunk.

The mule's name was Saladin, and in any contest of a mile or more Dex was positive he could not be bested by anything alive and operating on four legs. And he wasn't really quite convinced that Saladin would not outrun a hawk in the air or a steam engine on the ground if that was what he was asked to do. Saladin was no sprinter coming off the mark, but if he was given room to stretch out he would put the wind-roar in a man's ears and hold his speed long after a horse would falter and flag.

The only problems Dex foresaw in depending upon Saladin to finance his and James's travels would be when it came to convincing someone to strike a match against him. And that was where slow but flashy Galahad came in.

"There's no grain here," James complained when he inspected the feed bin. "The hay is bright and clean, but there's no grain."

"Tell you what," Dex said. "I'll clean his feet and brush him down. You go down to the livery and get a little grain. Not too much though. He won't be getting much use for the next few days, and we don't want to get him all heated up." He grinned. "And we sure don't want to take him out in public for a workout."

James grinned back at him. It would not do for anyone locally to see how fast Saladin was. "What d'you think? A quart each feeding?"

"That sounds good to me."

"It might take me a little while to get back. I want to stop and buy something to eat for myself too while I'm out."

"You didn't get breakfast?"

"Oh, they fed me, all right. Gave me a tiny little bowl with some hominy in it and a cup of coffee without any milk or sugar to put in it."

"Those sons of bitches," Dex said.

"Damn right," James agreed. "I'm still hungry."

Dex gave him a solemn look. "Hell, I don't care about that, darky. What I'm complaining about is that they charged me fifteen cents for your meal. Cheap bastards."

"Here, white boy." James tossed a curry brush to—or more correctly "at"—Dex with a hard, underhand throw. Dex was barely able to react in time to avoid having it thump into his belly. "Make yourself useful while I go fetch the groceries."

"You have money?"

James patted his belly and winked. "I wouldn't leave it in that room. Not likely."

"Good."

James glanced around to make sure they were not being observed by any strangers, then lifted his shirt and dipped two fingers into the rather well-stuffed money belt he wore. James customarily carried the bulk of their funds while Dex held only whatever amount they thought he might require for their immediate needs, this on the theory that any highwayman who might waylay them would certainly expect a gentleman to have money but would likely ignore the poor black servant who accompanied him.

"Need anything?" James asked.

Dex thought about that for a moment. He tilted his head back and stared absently toward the roof of the shed while he mused aloud, "You could fetch back a nice carriage for me. With yellow wheels, I think. And some French brandy. That would be nice. And a lamp. Something tasteful, like with naked ladies painted on the globe. Yeah, a lamp, I think. And a . . ."

Dex turned to see if James was getting all of this down, but he needn't have bothered. James had already left to complete his errands.

· 6 ·

Saturday was a fine day for a horse race. Warm without being too hot. Lacy, lumpy plates of cloud drifting high in an otherwise clear and brilliant sky. There was no sign of rain, which was a blessing. Saladin was at his best on dry turf.

Whitcomb and Grady Moore met them by prearrangement in front of the bank building at ten o'clock sharp. The gents wore cutaway coats and bright-colored vests in honor of the sporting occasion. They were riding together in an aged but well maintained landau. Dex and James were, of course, mounted.

Dex leaned down from his saddle to shake each gentleman's hand and said, "I hope you'll fill me in on the customs you observe. May I assume one needn't ride his own animal in the actual race, sir?"

Whitcomb laughed. "Good lord, yes. We all use jockeys. Not professional riders most of them, although I suppose a few could qualify as that. Mostly we use our own stable help or favorite local lads."

"Good," Dex said. "I'd rather have my man here ride for me if it's all the same to you."

"Of course," Whitcomb said.

Moore gave James a looking over and said, "It doesn't
look like you will be gaining any weight advantage by putting the nigra up. But it's always excitin' to watch, isn't
it?"

"Sometimes too exciting if you ride," Dex said.

"That's right, suh. Better to risk the nigger's neck than
your own."

James sat silent on Saladin, acting as if he hadn't heard.

"If you would lead the way, gentlemen . . ." Dex suggested.

Whitcomb nodded to his driver, an old man with leathery
brown skin, Mexican, or so Dex guessed. The driver took
up the slack in his lines and clucked softly, and the pair of
grays stepped out smartly, the sudden movement snapping
Whitcomb's and Moore's heads back.

Dex rode beside the landau to facilitate conversation.
James and Saladin dropped back and trailed along behind
at a distance great enough to avoid the billows of dust
raised by the passage of horse hoofs and wagon wheels.

Dexter was not particularly impressed by the grounds of
what Tyler Whitcomb referred to as a gentlemen's club.
They had better than this back home. Well, in what used
to be home until certain small difficulties convinced Dex it
was time to broaden his horizons and depart from Louisiana—quickly.

Here the gentlemen of Benson had very little in the way
of permanent structure. The course was natural turf with
only a long, oval-shaped line of waist-high, white-painted
stakes to mark the route. There was no railing, and the
stakes were only thin lathing strips hammered into the
earth. Dex didn't much care for that. Probably their theory
was that the wooden sticks were light enough to readily
snap off if a horse came too far inside and ran through
them, but light or not they could present a danger. A permanent heavy rail would have been much more to his lik-
ing. And there was no outside boundary at all. He supposed
a horse would be allowed to run as wide as it pleased so
long as it did not trample through the crowd.

There was, he had to admit, a fair turnout of men and even a few ladies present to observe the day's activities.

Several vendors had set up booths or small tents where pastries, lemonade, sweetmeats and more potent potables could be obtained.

There were no grandstands, but a permanent arbor framework had been erected and sometime over the past few days someone had gone to the trouble of cutting fresh brush to weave into the overhead latticework to give shade. The leaves on the brush were still green and scarcely wilted.

The women present were all gentlewomen, Dex observed. He was sure of this because the great majority of them were bog ugly, and a gentleman of any degree of taste or breeding would only permit himself to be seen in the company of an ugly woman if she were his wife or a family member.

He guessed there were upwards of a hundred people present, including a dozen or so women.

That was not, of course, counting the servants who were present to tend to the horses, wait on the gentry and remain otherwise invisible. James played his role as valet, stable boy and general dogsbody without needing any prompting. He held Galahad's head while Dex dismounted, then led both horse and mule away toward a long, stout picket rope where the other animals and servants were lined up well away from the festive gathering of east Texas swells.

Dex waited for Whitcomb and Moore to alight from the landau and then walked with them to join the others.

As he came closer to the crowd he began to smell smoke. His first thought was that the arbor had caught fire. Then he realized that the smoke was aromatic. Deliciously so.

"What the . . . what is it that I can smell cooking, sir?"

Whitcomb grinned. "Barbecue. Been turning half a beef on a spit since sometime last evenin', Mr. Yancey. You don't recognize it?"

"Recognize it, sir? I'm sure I've never encountered it before."

"In that case, Mr. Yancey, you are in for a treat. Barbecue is a tradition hereabouts. We couldn't have any sort of proper gatherin' without one. Why, sometimes I think the horse racin' is mostly an excuse to have the barbecue. We'll visit a spell first, then help ourselves t' dinner. The racin' won't begin until afternoon. In the meantime, Mr. Yancey, we'll have to see can we line up a suitable match for you and that fine horse o' yours.''

"You are very kind, sir.''

"It's my pleasure, suh. And will be all the more so when I put some of your money into my pocket.'' He laughed. The man also, Dex knew, meant the sentiment quite sincerely.

But then everyone knows what they say about even the very best of intentions.

• 7 •

Dexter was in love. In a state of lust too, but that was another subject entirely. Love, he was convinced, was the only proper term to apply to a newfound appreciation for the odd but undeniably delightful Texas dish—tradition, Whitcomb insisted—that was called barbecue.

The meat was ordinary enough, really. Excellent but ordinary, consisting of a smallish beef slow roasted over coals on a spit that was kept in more or less constant motion throughout a night and half a day as well. What made the Texas dish excel was the reddish brown, sweet and faintly tangy dipping sauce that accompanied the fork-tender shreds of beef.

Dex had no idea what ingredients might have gone into the dipping sauce, but he was thoroughly in favor of the result. Texas barbecue, he believed, could turn him into a trencherman of the first order.

Nor was there anything lacking when it came to the flowers of Texas femininity.

The wives were as homely as might be found back home in Louisiana, he thought, or perhaps even worse.

But at least a few of the younger ladies . . .

There was one—he hadn't yet had an opportunity to

make her acquaintance—who was really quite delectable.

She had flaming red hair, dimpled cheeks and cupid's bow lips. Her skin was so delicate and fair as to seem translucent. And she had a sprinkling of freckles across the bridge of her nose that Dex thought entirely fetching.

He couldn't help wonder if freckles were present on other portions of her anatomy. An anatomy which was, he thought, rather nice if one's preferences ran toward the lean and willowy.

Actually, Dex's preferences ran strong toward that which was available, whatever shape or form it might be in.

A pretty face and a comely ankle—he did admit to one prejudice, that being a distaste for thick ankles—and he asked for no more whether the lady was plump, squat or skeletal. Marvelous creatures, women. And this one more so than most. Sometime before this day was ended, he determined, he would have to find a way to meet her.

Still, there was also business to tend to.

He circulated among the gentry of Benson. Met. Smiled. Visited. Shared beverages and anecdotes, some of which were actually true. All in all it was a rather pleasant affair.

And by the time the al fresco dining was done and the assemblage was ready to get down to the entertainments of the afternoon, Dex had found five different gentlemen, Tyler Whitcomb first among them, who were willing to back their convictions with cash money.

The noble Galahad was scheduled to be run in the final race of the meet, the ritual culmination of the event being a two-mile run—twice around the track—with entry by invitation only and that limited to the best of the mature horses present.

"No horses under the age of five," Whitcomb explained. "The distance is too hard on the legs for younger animals, you see."

"I agree heartily," Dex told him. Galahad, poor thing, was seven.

"Our usual custom is that a horse must have proven itself already in order to earn an invitation to the last race. I spoke with the others after I saw your fine animal, though. They are in agreement with me, Mr. Yancey. Your mount is welcome." Whitcomb smiled. "So is your money, of course."

"You presuppose a victory, I take it," Dex said with an answering grin. "But then we all do, don't we? Otherwise there'd be no point in running the races."

"You accept our challenge then?"

"I do, sir."

"Excellent. I'll tell the others. With your horse the field will be six. Is that all right with you?"

"Throw every horse here onto the track at once, it's fine by me. I intend to go away this evening with my pockets heavy."

"Yes, well, we shall see, my boy. We shall see."

Dex glanced past Whitcomb's shoulder. The lady with the red hair was passing by. He thought about asking the banker for an introduction but before he had a moment in which to do so the woman—she was scarcely more than a girl actually, in her early twenties at the very latest—was greeted by a middle-aged gentleman Dex had met earlier in the day. His name was Mullen, and he'd been introduced as Whitcomb's partner at the bank.

The redhead greeted Mullen by rising onto tiptoes and planting a brief peck onto the gentleman's cheek.

Which answered at least part of his question, Dex thought. Her name would undoubtedly prove to be Mullen, and she would be the man's daughter.

That was all right. Dex had no prejudices against a pretty girl being wealthy too.

He would have said something to Whitcomb about the girl, but that gentleman excused himself and hurried away to catch up with someone else.

Dex was willing to bide his time. And meanwhile, he thought, he could profitably use the leisure to line up a few more wee wagers on the outcome of the final race of the day.

• 8 •

They'd scheduled five races for the day. After the fourth Dex nodded cheery hellos to the people he passed—he'd managed introductions to most of the folk in attendance but not yet to Miss Mullen—and made his way off to the picket line where James was waiting.

"He all ready?" Dex asked.

"Far as I know." James grinned. "I didn't want to try him out just yet, you understand. It wouldn't exactly do for somebody to see your boy perform his little trick too soon."

"No, I suppose it wouldn't."

"Is it time?"

Dex nodded. "Take him out into the middle of the track for his warm-up. We wouldn't want anyone to miss the performance now, would we?"

James chuckled and turned to Galahad. The handsome horse was carrying James's old military saddle, lighter in weight than Dex's comfortably padded plantation-style saddle. James hopped onto the horse and reined him toward the oval racecourse where other runners in the final event were already beginning to warm up, their jockeys maneuvering back and forth in front of the crowd in the time honored method of showing off . . . and increasing both the excitement and the betting.

Dex walked alongside James and Galahad until they reached the line of beribboned stakes that marked the outer edge of the course. James took the horse on alone from there.

"Fine looking animal," Dex heard from his side. Tyler Whitcomb had joined him unnoticed.

"Yes, he is, thank you. Which is your horse, sir?"

Whitcomb pointed toward an exceptionally tall but otherwise quite undistinguished brown.

"He's . . . very nice," Dex said, having to reach for something complimentary to say. In truth there was nothing in the brown's appearance to recommend him for speed or anything else.

Whitcomb laughed. "I know as well as you do what you're seeing out there, Mr. Yancey. Not much, that's what. But then the proof is in the running and not the parade. Or so I understand it."

Dex bowed to the gentleman and smiled. "As gentle a rebuke as I've ever received, Mr. Whitcomb. My compliments, sir."

"I like you, Yancey. 'Deed I do."

Out on the track Whitcomb's jockey put the brown into a canter and then briefly into a run. The horse had a fluid, easy stride. Paying more attention to it now, Dex also saw that Whitcomb's horse had a broad chest and unusually large, flaring nostrils. The combination would allow the brown to take in huge quantities of air, and that bespoke an animal with staying power. The length of its legs and the ease of its gait hinted as well that the brown might well have speed to go with its stamina: a formidable combination indeed.

Dex cocked his head to the side and examined the brown more closely. "I am beginning to see, sir, why you are so confident of victory."

"Would you care to increase your wager then?"

Dex pondered the offer for a moment. Then nodded. "I believe that I would, sir."

"You're on, young man. Prepare to pay."

"Only if you win," Dex chided.

"Oh, I wouldn't expect you to fork over until the formalities are done with," Whitcomb told him. "Oh, damn," the gentleman blurted.

"Pardon?"

"Look. Dammit all, anyway." Whitcomb pointed out into the middle of the course. James had started Galahad's warm-up. And the handsome creature had come to a slow, limping walk.

"Excuse me," Dex said hastily and dashed out onto the track to meet James.

He winked as he approached horse and rider.

"Everything all right?"

"Couldn't be better," James said happily. His tone of voice said one thing but his expression was frowning and severe. His eyes flicked past Dex toward the crowd, and in a slightly louder voice James whined, "It wa'n't my fault, bawss, I sweah, suh. Don' hit me, suh, please don'. I didn' do nothin't' hùrt this Gal'had ho'se, I promises you."

"Don't overdo the cornpone, you idiot," Dex whispered.

"Cain't be he'ped, bawss. I din' hurt him none, honest I din'."

Tyler Whitcomb and several of the other gentleman came near. Dex held Galahad's head while James slipped off the saddle and stood humbly quiet, his eyes downcast and his expression doleful.

"What seems to be the problem, Mr. Yancey?" a man named Forest asked.

"He must have turned an ankle on a clod or something. I really couldn't say."

"You there, boy. Walk him out and back again for us."

"Yezzuh, bawss, yezzuh." James led Galahad straight away. The horse walked with no trace of a limp.

"He looks all right now," Forest said.

Dex motioned James back onto the horse. "Try him again."

James mounted, reined Galahad away and, holding his crop low against his thigh so that its tip lightly touched

Galahad's right flank, kneed the horse into a walk.

Galahad moved off readily enough, but he walked with a pronounced limp on his left fore.

"Damn," Whitcomb mumbled.

"Get off him and bring him back this way," Dex called out.

James obediently dismounted and led Galahad back to the gentleman. The horse moved with no trace of discomfort.

"Nothing serious," Whitcomb said. "But he's in pain when he has the weight of a rider on him. What a pity. I was really looking forward to taking your money, Yancey."

"Personally I was looking forward myself to the pleasure of the match," Dex answered. And smiled. "I wouldn't have minded emptying your wallet for you either." He turned his attention to James. "Get back on and try him again, boy."

"Yezzuh." Once again though, when James mounted the horse walked with a distinct limp.

"No, better get off. He just can't take your weight until that ankle has a chance to rest."

"Yezzuh." James slid down to the ground.

"Damned shame, that's what it is," Whitcomb complained.

"Gentlemen, I have a thought. If you would all be so kind as to indulge me. I truly would hate to leave without the pleasure of running against you nice folks. Would you allow me to offer a substitute runner?"

"What d'you mean, sir?"

"I've made my wagers, gentlemen, and I would be ashamed to ask to withdraw them. But in truth, sirs, I'd like at least the opportunity to field a runner so as not to feel completely foolish afterward. Would you gentlemen consider giving me a chance to run another animal against you?"

"What is it that you have in mind, Mr. Yancey?"

Dex hesitated. Then he sighed. And told them.

◆ 9 ◆

A titter ran through the crowd as the horses came to the starting line. Horses, that is, and one lone mule.

The pale yellow mule looked as out of place among the sleek thoroughbred horses as a horse apple in a fruit salad.

James wasn't helping matters. He'd found a cap somewhere that was tattered and ancient and four sizes too big for him. He had it pulled down onto his ears and compounded that with a silly, vacuous expression. He'd even plucked a stem of grass and held it clenched in his teeth. Dex decided he was going to have to speak harshly with James about overdoing it.

Still, he couldn't possibly have looked any more awkward or stupid.

Saladin, of course, had no idea that he was an object of ridicule. The mule placidly ambled along with the others to the line of white lime that was the starting point. The mule's ears flapped and turned like flags in the wind, and his ratty excuse for a tail twitched futilely at some pesky flies.

Titters turned to outright laughter, and someone—Dex thought the man's name was Reckoner—was bold enough to nudge Dex in the ribs with an elbow and ask, "Say now,

Louisiana, are you sure you wouldn't like to add to your wager?''

"D'you have something to say about Louisiana, sir?''

"Only that in Texas we have more pride than to show off a . . . thing like that one.''

"You have a horse running, do you?'' Dex snapped.

"As a matter of fact I do, yes. The chestnut there with the star and snip.''

"Would you accept a side bet then? My mule against your chestnut, star and snip and bloody all?''

The Texas man frowned. "I say now . . .''

"Answer me, sir. Will you accept the wager from a Louisianan? Or will you back water?''

"All right, damn it. If you want to put it that way, fine. My Antigone versus your . . . whatever it is. Head to head, regardless of what any other animal does. Will that satisfy you?''

"At what price, sir?''

"Five hundred,'' the Texan said with no effort to disguise a sneer.

"Done,'' Dex declared. He heard a gasp from someone nearby.

"Mr. Yancey, it isn't really necessary for you to, um . . .''

"No, this man was rude enough to challenge me. Let's see if he is man enough to stand by his claims after the race is run, shall we?''

The fellow who'd tried to intercede bowed and withdrew several paces to show he was taking no sides.

"Your name is Reckoner, is it?''

"Reggoner,'' the gentleman corrected. "Charles Bordice Reggoner.''

"Very well, sir. I shall see you after the race.''

"Indeed you shall,'' Reggoner hissed, then turned away.

Out on the track the horses—and lone mule—were settling at the start line. The jockeys rode with shortened stirrups so they could put their weight well out onto the horses' withers where it would interfere least with the flow of balance and muscle in motion. All of them, that is, save

James, who rode bolt upright, looking and acting for all the world like a fencepost-dumb black boy with not a thought nor a care.

Dex sighed. He hoped James wasn't having *too* much fun at the expense of these Texans.

The starter checked to make sure that all the animals were standing quiet and square. Then he raised his fist high into the air, the slanting late afternoon sunlight gleaming on a small pistol there.

White smoke billowed from the muzzle of the pistol and moments later the sharp crack of the gunshot reached the spectators.

By then the line of horses—and one lone mule—were already surging into motion.

• 10 •

As far as Dex was concerned the race itself was little more than a formality. James kept Saladin at the rear of the pack, striding nice and easy, his long legs gobbling ground so smoothly that it scarcely seemed he was hurrying.

The one worry Dex'd had was that Saladin might get boxed in among the horses and, with no rail to guide on, be bumped inside the line of stakes that marked the course. That would have been grounds for disqualification, and that would have been a disaster.

He and James had discussed the danger beforehand, though, and James kept the mule well clear of the others. He trailed just behind the field through the entire first circuit around the mile oval, then began taking him around on the outside at the first quarter pole.

There were five runners other than Saladin, but Dex's judgment was that there was only one capable of offering any serious competition. That was Tyler Whitcomb's fine stallion, which took the lead immediately off the mark and set a blistering pace that the others gamely—and rather foolishly—tried to match.

Dex could see readily enough Whitcomb's strategy. And no doubt it worked right well in this normally uninspired company of country runners. Sprint early. Tire the competition. Then lope home with the others gasping and paddling in the rear.

Whitcomb's only miscalculation was that he had no idea what sort of opponent he faced in the yellow mule.

When the field was beginning to labor, Saladin was just getting warmed up.

As the horses cleared the quarter pole, James moved Saladin out and urged him forward. The big mule responded with heart and muscle alike, stretching his legs and flowing smoothly by the field, passing all except Whitcomb's powerful brown horse.

At the half mile Saladin was running on the brown's shoulder. Whitcomb's jockey, a wizened little Mexican with a mustache almost as large as the rest of him, glanced back, saw the challenge and responded with the whip.

The brown horse was not much to look at, but in motion it was a creature of grace and beauty. It responded with a surge forward that left Saladin with clods in his face from the brown's flying hoofs.

A pang of worry clutched at Dex's belly. Then eased as James calmly leaned forward onto Saladin's withers and tapped the mule lightly with his crop. One sharp slap and Saladin's ears snapped flat against his bony skull. His nostrils flared and he fairly leaped ahead.

Saladin caught the brown as they rounded the final turn and straightened out toward the finish.

By the end it was the brown horse that had to blink away the clods in its eyes. Saladin came home a length and a half ahead of Tyler Whitcomb's brown.

Dex grinned.

From the crowd around him there was a thunderous . . . silence.

And then, belatedly, a rousing cheer from the throats of those few gentlemen who truly appreciated speed and excellence when they saw it.

Charles Reggoner's Antigone, he of the chestnut coat with star and snip, came in a sweaty and ragged fourth place among the six runners, Dexter noticed.

All in all, he thought, it hadn't been a bad race.

• 11 •

Dex thought that B. Tyler Whitcomb was going to tear his arm off . . . with hearty congratulation. The banker was the first and the most vociferous to greet Dex after the race, rushing to him, grabbing his hand and pumping it vigorously and long.

"What a race! What a race!" Whitcomb exclaimed over and over again. "Magnificent. Wonderful. I never saw a better," he declared.

Dex grinned. "I take it you aren't angry?"

"Angry? Whatever for? It was a marvelous run." Whitcomb laughed. "To think. A mule." He laughed again. "But of course you were right. You did have to arrange the entry as indeed you did. We wouldn't have considered allowing you to enter that magnificent animal any other way."

"You aren't angry about that either?"

"Of course not. Oh, mark me, sir, I would have been quite upset had there been any hanky-panky with the running of the race. I'd not countenance anything like that. But your animal ran better than mine. He deserved the victory and never mind how you managed to get him onto the track. But tell me, please. If you don't mind, Mr. Yancey.

One gentleman to another. That racy looking thoroughbred of yours . . . ?''

Dex grinned. ''Galahad couldn't come in ahead of a wagon, Mr. Whitcomb, even if he was the horse that was pulling it.''

Whitcomb threw his head back and roared with laughter, quite enjoying the fact that he himself had been gulled. ''And the limp, sir?''

''Promise you won't tell anyone?''

''My word on it, Mr. Yancey.''

''The horse used to be owned by a young woman. God knows why, but she taught him his trick. If the rider . . . he doesn't do it unless there is someone up . . . if the rider touches his right flank with the crop, the horse limps on his left forefoot. If you touch the left flank, he limps on the right forefoot instead. When I learned that, from a gentleman who'd bought him thinking to race him, I had to have him. I suspect you can appreciate why.''

''Capital, absolutely first class,'' Whitcomb declared. He reached for his wallet. ''You said you would have my money, Mr. Yancey, and so you shall. But I must say, I count this as money well spent. I haven't had the pleasure of seeing such a race in I can't remember how long. If ever.''

Whitcomb cheerfully handed over the amount of his wager and even insisted on buying Dexter a drink to go with it. The gentleman also summoned the driver of his landau and ordered the man to take a stout drink and a plate of food to ''Mr. Yancey's nigra over there'' in appreciation for the job he'd done.

The other gents who'd taken wagers against Dex also were quick to seek him out and pay over the money they'd lost.

Save for one.

One man was conspicuously absent, Dex noticed after a while. Charles Reggoner was nowhere to be found.

Dex eventually caught sight of the fellow, standing well out of the way in the shade of the arbor in the company of

Tyler Whitcomb's partner, Mullen and the gorgeous red-head Dex had been admiring all day long.

If nothing else, Dex thought, bracing Reggoner—besides being a pleasure in and of itself—would give him an excuse to make the acquaintance of Mullen's beautiful daughter.

He excused himself from the group of excited race-goers with whom he'd been visiting and made his way through the crowd to plant himself square in front of Charles Reggoner.

He bowed first to Mullen and the young lady. "With your permission?"

"Eh? Permission 'bout what, Yancey?" Mullen responded.

"Mr. Reggoner and I have some business, sir." Dex graced the redhead with his very best smile—when he really worked at it he could produce a smile that would warm a matron's heart and make their daughters turn moist in the most intimate of places—and bowed again. "I apologize for the intrusion, miss, particularly so since we haven't yet been introduced."

Hat in hand and charm ratcheted to its highest level, he was awaiting the obligatory responses from Mullen when Reggoner butted in.

"I owe you nothing, damn you," the man hissed.

Dex was astounded. He gaped. Blinked. Straightened up and turned his attention away from the redhead.

He hadn't paid all that much attention to Reggoner before. Now he did so. And did not overmuch care for what he saw. Reggoner was probably in his early to mid thirties, slightly above medium height and well muscled. He was clean shaven and wore a silk hat and cravat—a rather tastelessly gaudy one, Dex decided now—and lacquered pumps under spotless spats. How the man had managed to spend an entire day trudging about on turf without soiling his footwear was something Dex marveled at. A fop, no doubt, he decided critically. Probably carried a lace hanky in his sleeve too. Dex sniffed in disdain.

"The wager, sir, was yours. The winnings, sir, are now mine. I will thank you to pay over or be damned."

Reggoner bristled and drew himself up to full height. "I owe you nothing. You're a charlatan and a cheat. And you are no gentleman."

"If I were not a gentleman, sir, you would now be flat on your ass." Dex remembered himself in time to give the young lady a smile. "My apologies, miss."

He was looking at the redhead and very nearly missed seeing the fist that came whistling in the direction of his jaw. Dex caught the movement out of the corner of his eye and barely had time enough to snatch his head back out of the way so that the unexpected punch swept harmlessly past.

Instead of engaging in a public brawl, Dex stepped backward a careful two paces and then very loudly announced, "I will take that as a challenge, sir, one that I am fully prepared to answer. Please designate a second to receive my terms."

"Whoa, now. Dammit, boys, whoa," Mullen said, stepping forward to place himself between the two younger men. "No one said anything here 'bout a challenge."

"With all respect, Mr. Mullen, you yourself have heard this man impugn my honor and assault . . . excuse me, but I should correct that . . . you saw him rather childishly *attempt* to assault me. I can interpret that no other way, sir, than as a deliberate challenge."

"Charles?" Mullen demanded.

By then Tyler Whitcomb had seen and rushed to join them. Whitcomb pressed close to Dex, a hand splayed lightly in front of his chest as if the older gentleman intended to hold Dex back by main force if necessary. "What is going on here, George?" Whitcomb asked, obviously directing the question to his partner.

"This . . . gentleman . . ." Mullen managed to make the word sound as if it tasted bad when it came off his tongue, "pressed a demand for money against Charles. Charles tells us he owes nothing and will not pay."

Whitcomb gave Reggoner a withering look. Or at least one that should have withered him. It did not. "I happened to overhear Charles's offer of a wager, George. I also heard young Yancey's acceptance of it. It was a side bet. Charles's Antigone against the yellow mule. Head to head and the faster animal wins. Well, the faster animal did indeed win. I would say that Charles owes Mr. Yancey for the loss. The stake, if I remember correctly, was in the amount of five hundred dollars. Is that correct, Mr. Yancey?''

"You know that it is, sir."

"I'll be damned if I pay any amount to this . . . this . . . *person*," Reggoner spat.

"George, Mr. Yancey, excuse us for a moment, please." The banker nodded to each gentleman, then took Reggoner firmly by the elbow and led him out from under the shelter of the arbor and a good distance off. Whitcomb's demeanor was intense as he placed his nose within inches of Reggoner's beetling brow and dark-red flushed face.

It was apparent that Charles Reggoner was not enjoying the tongue lashing he was receiving. But he had little choice except to stand and listen. Whitcomb ended by jabbing Reggoner several times on the breastbone with an extended forefinger.

Reggoner said something in response, and Whitcomb went at him again, this time rising onto his toes and repeatedly stabbing the younger man with the tip of that finger.

Finally Whitcomb calmed down and backed away half a step. A scowling and furious Reggoner whirled and stalked away at a pace just barely short of being a run. He headed for the picket line and disappeared from view.

Tyler Whitcomb returned to the arbor. "I hope you will be kind enough to accept my apologies, Mr. Yancey."

"Sir, no apology from you is necessary," Dex responded formally. "You are a true gentleman, and I have nothing but the utmost respect for you."

Whitcomb harrumphed and looked slightly embarrassed. "Yes, well, I've, uh, had a word with Charles." He managed a small smile. "Several of them, actually. If you would not mind the inconvenience, sir, please stop by the bank to secure your winnings. The funds will be available

to you there at any time you please from the opening of
business hours on Monday.''

Dex bowed to the gentleman. Tyler Whitcomb was indeed a gentleman, he thought.

''Uh, Tyler . . . ?''

''Later, George. We will discuss this later.''

Whitcomb's partner quite obviously did not care for the
arrangement Whitcomb just described, but there was nothing he could do about it now without making matters worse.
He glowered but gave in to the inevitable, took the red-
haired woman roughly by the wrist and dragged her away
without offering apology or words of parting to Dexter.

George Mullen, Dex thought, was nowhere near Tyler
Whitcomb in class or bearing.

But then not too many were in these modern times.

''I hope you will be good enough, Mr. Yancey, to withdraw your challenge. You have every right to press it, of
course. I do not dispute that. But . . . if I may ask a favor
of you?''

Dex bowed to the gentleman. ''Please, sir. My friends
call me Dexter. It would be an honor if I could count you
among them. And I shall be pleased to grant any favor you
would ask of me. We'll consider the matter closed, shall
we?'' He smiled.

So did Whitcomb. ''May I buy you another drink, Dexter?''

''If I remember correctly, sir, it is my privilege to stand
treat this time.''

''Now that is an offer I'll not turn down, Dexter.''

· 12 ·

Dex and James waited until they'd gotten back to the privacy of the hotel's horse shed before they clapped each other on the shoulders and burst into fits of happy laughter, each regaling the other with excited descriptions of a day at the races seen from two very different points of view.

"It couldn't have been better if I'd laid it all out in a script for each of them to follow," Dex declared, "right down to that asshole Reggoner with his loud mouth and big bank account, damn him. It will be a pleasure putting his money into our poke."

"You and your prissy white gentry," James returned. "You should have been back where all the fun was. These Texas boys know how to drink. Free, too. 'Course the white folk don't *know* they're providing all that they do. But then that's just part of the fun."

"I suppose you told the hired help how they ought to bet?" Dex asked.

James snorted. "Bunch of scared rabbits around here, let me tell you. I knew better than to give any of the jockeys the word, but I took a few of the grooms and hey-boys off to the side and whispered in their ears. Do you know something? There wasn't but one of them that trusted me far enough to bet like I said they ought. And me just as black as them.'' James clucked his tongue and shook his head sadly. ''Makes a body wonder just what this ol' world is coming to, don't it.''

''And the fellow who did bet on Saladin?''

James grinned. ''He is one happy nigger this evening, let me tell you.''

''How'd you make out yourself?''

''Wasn't much to take, but what there was is in the money belt right now. Forty-some dollars. How'd you do on the upper crust side of the tracks?''

It was Dexter's turn to grin. ''More than eight hundred, mostly thanks to Reggoner.''

James puckered his lips and emitted a low, long whistle. ''My oh my, can't we have fun on that much for a nice long time to come.''

''You bet your black ass we can.''

''Hand it over, white boy. I'll add it to the pile.'' James considered for a moment, then added, ''But I sure as hell hope you took it in currency 'stead of hard money. That much coin would slow me down if I have to jump out a window an' run from an irate husband.''

''You know me,'' Dex said. ''Always thinking ahead to critical moments just like that.'' The money he pulled out of his pocket and handed over to James was indeed paper currency, although it would have been entirely acceptable for him to demand the debts be paid off in large denomination coin. Not everyone in the south trusted paper money. But then in some places—Texas perhaps chief among them—the Reconstruction years had given the populace little reason to put their faith in the government or in anything it governed. The prejudices against paper money were part and parcel of that unpleasant legacy.

''Wait a second there,'' Dex said before James could cause the winnings to disappear inside his money belt. ''I'm gonna want some of that tonight. There's some serious celebrating to be done here.'' He took back a pair of twenties and slipped them into his pocket.

"Man, I could be drunk for two months on that much money," James said.

"So could I. But I have more interesting things in mind than that." He winked at his friend.

"Sounds like neither one of us is gonna have much need of the hotel room tonight," James said.

"You got something in mind too?"

"Oh, I expect maybe I'll find a little diversion."

"Pretty?"

"As a rosebud. And not much bigger. Tiny wee little bit of a bright-skinned girl with tits enough to share with two or three others just like her."

"One of the girls serving punch to the ladies today?" Dex asked.

"You noticed her?"

"Hell yes, I did. She's good looking. How'd an ugly son of a bitch like you get her eye?"

James laughed. "Funny thing how money in a man's pockets makes him handsome. And the more money he has, the better looking he gets."

"Just don't let her find out what you're carrying around your gut there, or her and half a dozen of her very closest friends may get ideas that we don't want them to have."

"Don't you worry, white boy. You know me. I always take care of business."

"You better or we're in the soup."

James stroked Saladin affectionately on the mule's scrawny neck. "Hell, we got nothing to worry about. Long as we got this old boy here we can always get more. Having him is kinda like owning the keys to the money store. We just walk in and pick out whatever looks good to us."

"It's like that for a fact, isn't it," Dex agreed.

"So which one d'you want to groom this evening?" James asked. "Saladin or your fine-looking shill over there?"

"You take Saladin. I'll do the horse. Got to keep you two children on good terms, you know. I'd hate for Saladin to sull up and quit running for you. Just keep him knowing that he's the smart one between you and everything will be all right.''

"Oh, he already knows that," James agreed with a smile. "What I'm scared he'll discover is sex. That would mess up his mind something awful, poor thing.''

"You know, maybe it woulda been better if I'd had you neutered back when I could have. It would've kept your mind focused.''

James faked a gasp and a shudder. It was a subject the two of them could comfortably joke about now, but there had indeed been a time in the past when Dexter or his father either one could have ordered James castrated and it would have been done.

"Hand me the curry comb, would you?" Dex asked as he turned his attention to grooming handsome—and amazingly useful—Galahad after the horse's not too difficult day of work.

· 13 ·

An evening spent in the company of George Mullen's lovely redheaded daughter would have been the perfect capper to an otherwise already near-perfect day.

It was also, unfortunately, quite impossible.

Circumstance and Charles Reggoner had combined to destroy Dex's one opportunity to make the acquaintance of the belle in question. Drat it.

Still, Dex's experience was that lightness of heart and gaiety of spirit come not from pining over what might have been but from embracing whatever is possible.

In this case, that meant spending no time mooning over a girl he hadn't met—yet—and pursuing instead one whose company he already knew he could and would enjoy.

He treated himself to an elegant—but light; it wouldn't do to find himself overfull and uncomfortable—supper, then ambled along the streets of Benson to a saloon and gaming club he'd found immediately after arriving in the community.

"Beer, mister?" the barman asked.

"What would you have in the way of a brandy?" Dex responded.

"Not a drop. You had the last of it the other evening when you was here then."

"Whiskey then?"

"Rye or bourbon."

"No Scotch?"

"Rye or bourbon."

Dex sighed. "Bourbon, if you please."

The bartender poured a generous measure from a bottle whose smeared and soiled label suggested it had been filled and refilled a few times too many. Dex handed the man a quarter and collected his dime in change, then carried his drink to a corner table.

He did not think he would have long to wait there alone, and he was right. He was soon approached by a blond girl who had youth on her side—he guessed her age at fifteen or sixteen—but who otherwise was fighting a losing battle in the pursuit of beauty. She obviously bought her powder and rouge by the pound, an investment that would have been better directed toward soap and towels. She was, however, subtle. "Want to fuck, honey?"

"Very kind of you to offer, I'm sure, but is Helena working tonight?"

The blond girl didn't bother to pretend a look of disappointment. "Who shall I say is calling?" Meaning, Dex gathered, that Helena might or might not be in a humor to make an appearance this evening, depending on the identity of her suitors.

"Dexter. Please tell her it's Dexter who would appreciate the pleasure of her company."

"Sure, honey. I'll tell her just that way, too." The blonde turned and went not upstairs to the rooms where the girls plied their trade but into the back of the place where a kitchen and storeroom might presumably be. She left behind her a lingering scent of toilet water and sour sweat. Dex wrinkled his nose and had a sip of the bourbon. That proved to be no help whatsoever. Sweat and toilet water were actually an improvement over the cheap bourbon they served here.

Fortunately he hadn't long to wait. Seconds after the

blonde disappeared into the back room the door burst open again and a smiling Helena came dashing in a beeline for Dex's table.

Ah yes, he thought.

Prospects for the evening were most definitely looking up.

· 14 ·

Helena kissed him deep and slow, her tongue exploring gently inside his mouth. He'd wondered if she might have quickly forgotten him. She hadn't.

"Lovely," he said.

"Me?" she asked. "Or that?"

"Both," he assured her. The word seemed to please her greatly. She sighed and kissed him again.

Some moments later, when Helena withdrew from his lips half an inch or so, Dex said, "You've changed your hair."

"D'you like it?"

"Very much."

"You mean that?"

"I do."

"Good. I was . . . d'you mind if I tell you somethin'?"

"I would be pleased to listen to anything you have to say, my dear."

"I was thinkin' to make myself pretty for you when I done this. Had it done, I mean. One o' the other girls helped me." She pulled further away and turned her head—she really was quite pretty—first this way and then that, posing before him and inviting his approval.

Her hair was a glossy and gleaming black, practically aglow with health and vitality. The first time Dex saw her it was long and worn in a bun that she'd been willing to loosen and let fall once she felt comfortable with him. Since then she'd had it trimmed to a much shorter length and made curly by some arcane and mysterious process that males were undoubtedly prohibited from understanding even if they'd been interested in such a subject.

"You really like it?" she persisted.

"I really like it," Dex affirmed.

That brought a smile to her face and she rewarded him with a kiss. Which led to another kiss. And then . . . it sometimes amazed Dex how time consuming a simple kiss can become.

Eventually Helena satisfied herself that Dexter both genuinely appreciated the hair style and that he truly didn't object to kissing. Both seemed to delight the girl.

Even so, she turned suddenly shy.

"What's wrong?"

"Nothing."

"All right. I'll accept that. Nothing is wrong. But you're thinking about something. What is it?"

She hesitated for a moment more, then confessed. "There's something . . ."

"Mmm?"

"I ain't never done it before."

"Oh?"

"The other girls've told me about it, see. But I never done it. They say the men like it awful good. Gets them extra pay. Not," she very quickly added, "that it's more money I'm wantin' from you, Dexter. It's just . . . with you it's almost like I'm a real person. You know?"

"Dear girl," he told her. "You are not only very real, you are very sweet. I like you. I enjoy my time with you. It pleases me to think that you like me too."

"With most guys . . . ah, I can't blame them. I'm a whore. That's the truth. I don't mind them thinkin' about me that way 'cause it's so. But with you . . . Dex honey, with you I almost forget that the reason we're together is 'cause I'm a whore. You want to know something?" This time she did not wait for a response before hurrying on to say, "If you're broke, honey, or are runnin' low, you just come to me anyhow. I won't charge you. Not a penny. I'll . . . I'll give your money back tonight too if you like."

And that, Dex thought, was as sincere and fine a compliment as ever in his life he'd received. He kissed the girl, first on the mouth and then very lightly on the tip of her nose. "As a matter of fact, dear, I am particularly flush this evening." He told her about the race.

"That was you won that race? Oowee, I sure heard about that." She laughed.

"Something funny about it?"

"Yeah, there is. But never mind that. I was gonna tell you something."

"Oh, yes. So you were. I'll be quiet and listen." He was quiet. But he wasn't completely inactive. He began toying with the tip of Helena's right nipple. It quickly became rigid and she started to squirm.

"Are you gonna listen to me or ain't you?"

"I am," he promised. But he continued to play with her nipple.

"What I was *tryin'* to say is about this thing that some o' the other girls do t' please a fella extra special. An' I know how you are about a girl's mouth, y' see . . ."

"Goodness," Dex said. "You said you've never done this thing before? Do you mean to tell me you've never had a gentleman's pecker inside that pretty mouth of yours?"

She slapped him lightly on the chest. "Dexter, get serious. O' course I suck cock, honey. Lordy, I expect I've taken more meat in my mouth than you've had t' eat your whole life long. I been drinking cum since I was, what? fourteen? 'Bout that long. No, o' course it ain't that. But there's one thing that, well, I never till now met any fella that I'd want t' please so much as I want t' please you."

"And this thing would be exactly what?"

She giggled. Then leaned forward to whisper low in his ear even though they were alone in the room with the door bolted and the one window hidden behind carefully drawn shades and heavy draperies.

Dex listened. Then grinned. "It's called 'going around the world', sweetheart. And yes, that would certainly please me very much."

"Then I want you t' roll over onto your tummy, Dex honey. I'll start at the nape o' your neck, an' if I go an' miss one single square inch you remind me where it is an' I'll go back an' see that it's taken care of proper."

Dexter had heard worse ideas in his time. He rolled over as instructed and allowed the pretty girl to have her way with him.

· 15 ·

Dex sighed. He felt quite thoroughly satisfied. Drained, as it were. And no wonder. Helena had proven to be *very* good at her chosen profession. Thoughtful too. Once she was satisfied that Dexter was—at least for the moment—completely sated, she plumped a pillow behind his neck and then slipped off the bed to pad barefoot and naked—very prettily so, even when seen from the rear—to the washstand.

She bathed her more private parts and went so far as to brush her teeth with salt and the stub of a willow trig before she came back to cuddle tight against Dex's side.

He kissed her.

Helena's eyes went wide. "You don't have to do that, honey. I mean . . . after what I been doing just now an' everything. You really don't."

"You don't like it?" he asked.

"You know that I do," she said.

He responded by kissing her again, knowing how much that simple act pleased her.

Helena kissed him back, very gently, and with a tiny murmur of contentment laid her pretty head on Dex's shoulder. "I never been with anybody as nice as you, Dexter. An' I mean that sincerely, I do."

"Thank you."

She gave him a quick hug and ran her tongue lightly down the side of his neck, then giggled when Dex began to squirm. "Are you ready again so soon, Dex honey?"

"Give me a little while yet. We aren't in any hurry."

"Sure. Whatever you want. You know I'd do most about anything for you, Dexter. I mean that, too. I really would."

"Oh, I do hope so, dear. I have some things in mind for, um, later on this evening."

"Good," Helena said emphatically. "D'you want to sleep first?"

"No, we'll just lie here and rest for a bit. I like having you close like this. Like being able to look at your body." He smiled. "Most girls look their best when they're dressed," Dex mused aloud, idly toying with the tip of Helena's left nipple while he did so. "You are at your prettiest when you're naked."

"I used t'be fat," Helena told him, turning slightly so he could more easily reach her other nipple.

"I don't believe that. Not for a minute, I don't."

"I sure as hell was, Dex honey. Fat." She made a face. "But kinda happy anyhow."

"I still don't believe it."

"Oh, I wouldn't lie to you, Dexter. I swear I wouldn't. Not never."

He kissed her lips and said, "I believe you, dear." Which of course he did not. There hadn't been a woman yet born, he believed, who would not lie to a man, and Helena would be no exception to that rule. But he was equally certain that at this particular moment in time Helena herself believed that broad but erroneous statement. So her intent was good even if her accuracy was slightly at fault. Besides, there was no harm in being agreeable. "I do believe you," he repeated. Repeated the kiss too, then lay back and enjoyed the warmth of Helena close against his side.

"I guess I was kind of a stupid kid," Helena nattered

on, chatting sleepily, perhaps in an effort to keep herself awake and available for him whenever he wished. "I was fat and didn't know squat about men and whoring and all like that. That was when things were good, you see. At home, I mean. My daddy, he was a good man. Engineer on a steam locomotive, that's what he was. He was real proud of that, too. We lived nearby the tracks and every run, he'd make a bunch of them every day most about, every time he passed the house he'd blow the whistle and wave. Didn't make any difference could he see mama or me in the yard or not, he'd know we could hear and he'd blow that whistle regardless.

"But then the lake dried up and the railroad shut down 'cause there wasn't any business anymore. No need for it then, of course. And daddy lost his job and couldn't keep mama and me the way he was used to, and it shamed him. It shamed him awful bad it did, and after a little while being broke he couldn't take it no more. He went out in the woods one day and shot himself in the head."

Helena made a small sound that Dex couldn't quite interpret. Then she said, "Poor stupid man. I guess I shouldn't ought to say that, but I know now that it's so. He got it wrong. Even shooting himself in the head, he didn't get it quite right. He . . . I don't know. He flinched or something, like at the last second, and he blowed half his face off with that old shotgun but he didn't kill himself. Not right off, he didn't. They carried him back to the house, and he laid there for the better part of a week before he finally up and died.

"That took the heart out of mama too, watching over daddy like that and seeing him die and knowing he'd done it his own self, that he'd decided to quit her and me and give up after the lake and the railroad was gone. Mama waited for daddy to finish dying, then she drank a big old dose of lye." Dex's eyes were closed but he could feel Helena shudder.

"I'd rather go like daddy did than mama. I was there with the both of them when they died, and believe me, she could've picked a better way than the lye. Anyhow, after that, I gaunted down pretty quick. Lost my baby fat and my illusions, too. Hadn't any schooling to speak of and didn't know jack-shit about the world. But once I started to lose some weight I wasn't so awful bad to look at, I guess, and some of the men came around and offered to educate me about the way things are. And so here I am.''

"I'm sorry about your folks, Helena," Dex said. "But to tell you the truth, I'm glad that you're here with me tonight.''

"Me too, Dex honey," Helena said in a brittle, patently false tone of professional gaiety.

The girl was quiet for a time, and Dex very nearly fell asleep. After a bit, though, something she'd said floated to the surface of his drifting thoughts, and his eyes snapped open.

"The *lake* went away? Is that what you said? Wherever could a lake go to? And who in the world would take it there?''

Helena laughed and hugged him. She seemed to be over her moodiness now. "Nobody took it, honey. It dried up. The Army Corps of Engineers said they were gonna improve it but they screwed everything up instead. Since then there's been no way to get the riverboats up there and the farmers have trouble shipping their crops. There's talk all the time about building a railroad, but nobody's ever really gone and done it though everyone wishes they would.''

She explained further. Much further. It was all more than Dexter particularly wanted to hear. Just saying that the damned lake dried up would have been quite enough, thank you. But the girl was a talker, and she talked on. Dex listened with only half an ear while Helena chattered on and on. And on some more.

Is there *any*thing, Dex wondered, that is quite so boring, quite so insufferably banal, as someone else's life story?

He yawned, teeth chattering as he tried to clamp his jaw closed to cover the yawn, and fought to stay awake through Helena's interminable dissertation. Not that he wanted to hear what the girl was saying. But he was commencing to feel the stir of renewed interest—and ability—low in his groin and did not want to drop off to sleep again lest he sleep right on through until morning.

His intention was to have another tussle with this willing and very adept lass, sleep until daybreak and then enjoy the pleasures of her . . . um . . . company again before parting. And immediate slumber would cut down on that schedule of activity, a state of affairs that he would much prefer to avoid.

So he listened—more or less—and considered the various possibilities of delight whilst he recuperated and prepared himself for a return engagement.

· 16 ·

"You look beat," James observed from the vantage point of a cot tucked away behind the wardrobe. As Dexter's servant—which he certainly was seen to be so far as the outside world was concerned—James would have been lynched had he presumed to overstep himself and sleep in a white man's bed. Actually, he was lucky to have been given a cot here. Most inns or waystations either required that he sleep in the barn with the horse and mule or, if Dex insisted that he needed his manservant's assistance through the night, reluctantly provided a pallet on the floor. A black man's comfort was not something that deserved consideration.

Dex grinned at him. "Beat," he agreed, "but happy."

"Have a nice time, did you?"

"Very." Dex frowned. "Come to think of it, you look awfully well rested this morning. I thought you had plans for last night."

James made a wry face, then smiled and shrugged. "Sometimes it's like that."

"She was pretty. I saw that for myself."

"Yeah, she was pretty. Great tits, too. But dumb?" He rolled his eyes. "Lordy, that poor little ol' gal couldn't've put two words together to make one sentence. Not if I'd spotted her 'I' or 'the' and offered suggestions.''

"Fine, but could she fuck? I thought that was the idea."

James frowned. "You have to do something to fill all that time between wrestling matches. That Betty girl, she was a disappointment."

"That's the price you pay for being an educated nigger. Kind of hard to find your equal."

"Just once I'd like to come across a girl I can talk to when we're finished screwing. You know?"

"Not me. I don't have that problem."

"Your girls are all smart?"

"You weren't paying attention. What I said was that I don't find it t'be a problem." Dex grinned, and James laughed and threw a pillow at him.

That set them off, and the two of them—fully grown men approaching thirty years of age and certainly old enough to know better—got into a whap, woolly, laugh and tussle pillow fight that only ended when they realized how loud they were getting and quit before some passerby in the hallway overheard and wondered what the hell the Louisiana gentleman and his "servant" were up to in there.

Dex was puffing and half out of breath when they stopped flailing each other with the pillows. No seams had come undone. But there were more than a few wisps of down floating in the still air, and the room seemed stuffy. "I win," Dex said, declaring a victory that he had not necessarily earned by way of combat.

"The hell you say."

"I always win. That's the rule." Dex chuckled. He wadded his pillow into a fluffy ball and tossed it at James.

James merely looked smug. In point of fact, he usually was able to outrun and outwrestle Dexter, although Dex could nearly always best him when it came to marksmanship, fencing and horsemanship. They were very well matched when they competed and had been for as long as either of them could remember.

Dex went to the window and opened it to let some fresh air in, then tugged on the control rod to tilt the transom open above the hotel room door. That meant they would have to assume whatever they said inside the room could be overheard and act accordingly, minding their manners and their places alike. It was a habit so ingrained over the years that neither had to consciously think about it now.

"Where's that razor, James?"

James silently left his cot and fetched soap and razor both for Dex's shave.

The same bowing and scraping old black man met Dex at the dining room door and led him to a choice table beside the window. He could have had any other had he preferred, though. Dexter was the only gentleman in the place on this Sunday morning.

"That black China tea fo' you again today, suh? An' does you want me to feed yo' man theah?"

"The China Black will be fine, uncle, and yes, I want breakfast for my man. Mind though. I've learned what a poor breakfast you serve in the back here though I pay a good price for his meals. I'll have no more of that. See to it that he gets a proper breakfast. Grits and gravy, perhaps some sausage or bacon. I expect full value when I pay for a meal." Dex knew that grits and gravy were one of James's favorites. Dex's too for that matter.

"Yes, suh. I will see to it myself, suh, I sho'ly will."

"Thank you, uncle."

The waiter picked up the napkin beside Dexter's place, carefully shook it out and draped it onto Dex's lap. "Will there be anything else fo' now, suh?"

"No, I'll peruse the menu while you tend to the other."

"Very good, suh, very good. I be back right away with yo' tea."

Dex was still looking at the menu, trying to decide between a cheese soufflé and the plebeian but delectable combination of biscuits and gravy when he heard a commotion in the kitchen and moments later James burst into the dining room at a run, his face a contorted mask of anguish and fury combined.

· 17 ·

"Dex! Come quick. My God, it's Saladin."

The old waiter drew back in horror at the too-familiar form of address from a black man to a white, but Dex had no time to worry about that. If James so forgot himself as to shout like that then something was plenty damn serious. Dex leaped from his chair and followed James out through the kitchen and into the trash-strewn yard at the rear of the hotel.

Together they ran to the shed where Saladin and the trick horse were stabled.

Had been stabled.

Now there was only the horse.

Saladin was there, all right. Or what had been the swift and gallant mule remained there.

The straw on the floor of his stall was awash with drying blood. The whole inside of the shed smelled of the sharp, coppery stink of it. A black scum had developed on the surface of the blood but there was so much of it that the drying hadn't penetrated throughout so that bright scarlet smears showed through beneath the darker surface.

Saladin's body, the yellow coat still gleaming with what should have been health and good grooming, lay against the far wall, wedged hard into the corner there as if he'd been trying to back away from whomever did this to him.

It took but a glance for Dex to see what had been done to the great-hearted creature.

Some son of a bitch had come in during the night and coldly, deliberately cut Saladin's throat.

"Jesus!" Dex blurted. He felt like crying. He looked at James and could tell that he too was as deeply disturbed.

And not only for the loss of their primary source of income. Dex had *liked* Saladin. It was that plain, that simple. Beyond the speed, beyond the stamina, he'd very much liked and admired the big mule's willingness of spirit. There had never been a time that Saladin gave less than his very best effort no matter how long the run or how weary he'd become. Saladin gave them his heart as well as his speed. He'd given everything and demanded nothing in return.

And now some vile and miserable piece of human putrefaction had done this to him.

In the stall next to Saladin's, the horse—Dex found that he no longer thought of the bay gelding by the name Galahad, which really had been intended only as a come-on to entice bettors into wagering against a mule—the bay horse was fidgety and nervous, no doubt from the stench of blood that permeated the atmosphere inside the shed.

"Look, I . . . Jesus, I don't know what we should do first. I guess first thing, you'd better take the horse out. Take him," Dex hesitated for a split second, trying to get over the shock of this discovery and work things out, "take him down to the livery stable. Tell them I'll be along later to arrange for his board there."

"What are you going to do, Dex?"

"I'm going to go find the sheriff or the town marshal or whoever the hell is in charge of the law around here."

James shuddered. But then his exposure to the ideals of law and justice had been rather different from Dexter's. "If you want my opinion, Dex, I'd say we go down to that livery and buy us another riding animal and then get the hell out of this town. Today. Right now. You don't want to wait that long, fine. You don't even have to come up with another saddle animal. I'd be willin' to walk to the next town, wherever that is."

"No," Dex said firmly. "We aren't leaving Benson. Not now we aren't." The small muscles beneath his jaw clenched and stood out sharply. "There's nothing could make me leave this place right now, James."

"Dammit, Dex, if folks hereabouts would do somethin' like this to a poor damned mule . . ."

"Nobody did this to a mule, James. Whoever the bastard was—and I pretty much have an idea who it would have been, who it almost has to've been—he did this to me an' he did it to you. I won't leave, James. Not now. Not on your life and not on mine."

"I don't think . . ."

"If you want to go on, I won't blame you. We can meet someplace else when I'm done here. Or if you'd rather we can split our poke right here and now and wish each other well. Whichever you prefer."

"Jesus, Dexter, I'm not going anyplace without you. That's not what I'm saying. I just . . . I don't like this place anymore. And that is the natural truth, I promise you."

"I don't like it either, James, but I'm not leaving. Not until the son of a bitch that did this pays for what he's done."

"Pays? You don't mean . . ."

"No, I don't mean money. Unless that's the thing he holds most dear. If he worships money then I'll take that from him. If he has a wife he dotes on, I'll take her. And if it's his own sorry life that he cares the most about then I'll want to see if I can get as much blood out of him as he's spilled from Saladin."

James stood there for a moment in silence, looking down at the dead mule and at the flies that were feasting around the grand animal's open mouth and lifeless eyes. "All right," he said finally. "All right."

James shuddered again, then turned and opened the gelding's stall. He slipped a headstall onto the horse and attached a lead rope to it. Moments later he led the horse out into the bright glare of the early-morning sunlight and away in the direction of Benson's livery stable.

Dex stood where he was until James and the horse were out of sight and then, his heart heavy and feeling as if he carried a lump of cold lead in his belly, he too turned away and went to ask where he could find whoever handled the lawing in Benson, Texas.

• 18 •

"The sherf, he ain't home, mister." The woman who'd answered Dexter's knock was a thin and bony, exceptionally dark-skinned Negress.

"I was told he would be."

"You was tol' wrong, mister."

"Louella. Who the hell is that at the door?" The bellow came from somewhere inside the house.

The black woman gave Dex an unapologetic look and moved aside only when the sheriff came stumping and blinking into the vestibule.

Sheriff Dan Mickens was of middle years and middle height. What he lacked in height, however, he more than made up for in heft. He had belly enough for a brood sow and graying beard stubble that made it clear he hadn't bothered to visit a barber shop in the better part of a week. His eyes were bloodshot and his teeth, the few he still had, were a darker shade of yellow than Saladin's coat had been.

The sheriff wore slippers made from pieces of faded carpet, shabby trousers that might once have been black and was shirtless except for a once-white union suit. He had one strap of a pair of galluses looped over his left shoulder to keep his pants up. The other strap dangled at his side.

All in all, Dex thought, the good sheriff gave the impression of a man coming off an extended drunk.

"Go 'way," the sheriff said.

"I need to talk with you, sir. It's a matter that needs the law."

"Tomorrow, boy." Mickens turned to the black woman and asked, "This's Sunday, i'n'it, Louella?"

"Yes, suh, this be the Lord's day fo' sure."

Mickens returned his attention to Dex, blinked several times and half-heartedly stifled a belch. The man's breath would have gagged a buzzard. "Tomorrow, I tol' you. Office hours aren't till tomorrow."

"This needs your attention now."

"Tomorrow," Mickens said. Without further ado he took a careful and slightly wobbly step backward and closed the door in Dexter's face.

Renewed knocking brought no response. After several unproductive minutes Dex turned and made his way back to the hotel. He needed further direction to find his way around the residential sections of town.

"I tol' you, dammit, that I . . . oh. It's you. Sorry, sir. I didn't mean to shout."

"I am sure you did not, Dan," B. Tyler Whitcomb said in an amiable and unruffled tone of voice. "And I must apologize for disturbing your Sunday rest."

"No bother, sir. No bother at all," the sheriff assured him.

"It is just that my friend Mr. Yancey here is the victim of a truly horrendous crime. Not the sort of thing we are accustomed to in our fair town, as I've already explained."

"No, sir, Mr. Whitcomb. Good folk hereabouts." He belched again but this time he kept the noxious fumes contained within a fist.

"Yes," the local gentleman agreed. "We are not used to crime, but I told him the community would respond quickly to bring justice to bear. That is the way you see things too, is it not, sheriff?"

" 'Deed it is, sir, 'deed it is. Always ready to leap to the call o' duty, sir."

Whitcomb bobbed his head and smiled just as nicely as if he believed that blatant falsehood. "Exactly what I've already told my young friend Yancey here, sheriff. I knew he could count on you."

"Yes, sir, Mr. Whitcomb. Always ready."

"Then if you would excuse me? I don't wish to be late for Sunday services." Whitcomb nodded, first to Mickens and then to Dex. He turned and hurried away in the direction of a white church steeple Dex could see towering above the town at a distance of several city blocks.

"Thank you, sir," Dex said as the banker departed.

He turned back to the sheriff who belched again, not bothering to cover it this time.

"I s'pose you're gonna want to tell me what's got you s' damn het up this morning," the sheriff accused.

"Yes, sir, I suppose that I am," Dex agreed with him.

•19•

"Jesus God, mister, it's only a damn mule." The sheriff made a face, peered into the stall where Saladin's body lay and spat a stream of tobacco juice without bothering to turn his head. The brown juice splashed onto one of the slim and seemingly delicate ankle bones that had carried Saladin with such wonderful speed.

The sheriff did not seem pleased to be there. But then neither was Dexter.

"It was *my* mule," Dex said, very careful to keep his voice under control. This dimwitted excuse for a Texas sheriff pissed him off, and that was the natural truth. It was equally true that further aggravating the man would accomplish exactly nothing.

"Mind, mister, I ain't pretending that doing this thing to your mule was all right. We don't put up with vandalism around here. No throwing stones at glass windows or none of that. But Jesus God, man. What d'you want me to do? Find the kids that done this and charge them with what— mule murder? I'm sorry as hell that this happened, but surely you ain't so hard up for the ten bucks or so that a mule is worth that you'd want to see some kid thrown in jail or his folks disgraced. Hell, mister, it's only a damn mule.''

Dex did not even consider making explanations to Mickens. And it was *not* some rowdy juveniles who'd done this. He was sure of that. Saladin's killing had been an act of pure, mean-spirited, cold-hearted revenge. Dex was as certain of that as he was certain that Sheriff Dan Mickens was an asshole. Both of those propositions, Dex figured, were absolute givens.

"What is it you're wanting me t'do, mister?" Mickens asked. He spat again, the fluid this time striking Saladin's hoof. There was no logical reason why that should bother Dex. Certainly the mule was beyond feeling anything. Wouldn't have felt a touch of moisture on a hoof if he had still been alive. But, dammit, the sheriff's indifference made Dex seethe all the more.

"I want you to find whoever did this and prosecute him."

Mickens spat again. Turned. Looked silently at Dex for several long moments. Then he shrugged. "Fine. I'll tell my deputies. We'll ask around. Investigate this here heinous crime right thorough. All right? Does that satisfy you?"

Dex bit back an impulse to express amazement that Mickens would know a word like "heinous" and nodded. "I would appreciate it." He wouldn't. Not any more than the sheriff and his deputies would actually investigate anything about the killing of a mere mule. But there was no point in going into all that now. It would only result in shouting and hard feelings. And those were not what Dexter had in mind.

"You know where my office is," the sheriff said.

"No, sir, I don't."

Mickens grunted and told him. "Regular hours are Monday to Friday. We got a deputy on duty Saturday nights too. He can't see everything or this wouldn't of happened to your mule. Thing is, you come by any time. There's somebody in the office seven ayem to six in the evening. You want to ask how we're coming along on this case, you just drop in whenever you want. O' course if we do make any progress I'll make it a point t' find an' tell you. Is that fair?''

"Yes, sheriff, that is entirely fair. Thank you."

"All right then. Now if you'll excuse me, I got things t' do at home."

"Thank you very much for coming, sheriff. Uh, there's one other thing though."

"Yes?"

"What do you want done about, well, the body?"

Mickens shrugged again. "Do whatever you want, mister. Or whatever Johnny wants."

"Johnny?"

"Tatum," the sheriff said, pointing over his shoulder with a thumb. "Owns the hotel. I don't expect he'll want a dead mule stinking up his place, so you'll want to move the sonuvabitch pretty quick before the smell gets bad."

Dexter sighed. Wonderful. Not only was Saladin dead, Dex very likely would have to pay someone to haul the carcass away. Finding someone to attend to that chore was not apt to be easy on a Sunday morning. "Thank you for all your help, sheriff."

"Any time. Sorry this happened, mister, but you come by the office any time you want, hear?" Come by the office. Implied but unstated was that further visits to the sheriff's house would not be appreciated and never mind that Dex was favorably acquainted with Benson's banker. Dex heard all right. And understood. He wouldn't waste any more effort trying to do things nice and legal around here. If anything were to be done about Saladin's killing it would have to be done by Dex and James themselves.

"Thank you, sir."

Mickens grunted. Spat—he hit only blood-soaked straw this time—and walked away, passing from the shed out into the sunshine and growing heat of the day.

• 20 •

Dex was pretty thoroughly pissed off by the time James came sneaking into the hotel room. It was almost midnight, and Dex hadn't seen or heard from James since early in the day when he'd taken Galahad off to the livery stable. Late in the afternoon Dex had gone there looking for him. Galahad was there all right, cozy in a clean stall, but there was no sign of James. Now James came tiptoeing in, shoes in hand and reeking of whiskey. Light a match too close in front of him, Dex thought rather sourly, and his breath would catch fire.

"Out drowning your sorrows, were you?" Dex accused.

"You're awake," James said.

"Damn but you're sharp when you're drunk. Yes, I'm awake."

"I was trying to be quiet so I wouldn't wake you."

"Don't bother. I wanted to see just how long you'd stay out partying when some son of a bitch has just ruined us."

"I wasn't partying. Well, okay, so I was. But not the way you think I was. Dammit, Dex, d'you really think I don't care about Saladin? And not just because he was our meal ticket either. I *liked* that mule, Dexter."

"So what the hell were you doing then?"

"Just a minute. Since you're awake anyway we might as well have a talk. Can you find the matches and get that lamp lighted? I don't want to bump into something and stub my toe."

Dex rather reluctantly felt around on the bedside night stand until he encountered the box of sulfur-tipped lucifers laid ready there, managed to get the fragile globe off the lamp without breaking it and struck the match. The flare of sudden light showed that James's shirt was in disarray and his eyes were bloodshot, but at least he wasn't falling all over himself. Dex touched the flame to the lamp wick, adjusted the thumbscrew until he got a nice butterfly of fire and shook the match out.

"Now what is it you want to talk about at this hour of the night?" He still felt—and sounded—a trifle peevish.

"I been doing some talking," James said.

"You've been doing some drinking, too," Dex accused.

"Yeah, I have. Been buying for everybody in sight and drinking a little myself as well. But it wasn't just to drown our sorrows. I been asking questions, Dex, and I bet I learned a lot more today than you did."

"How's that?" Dex sat up on the side of the bed and rubbed his eyes. He was sleepy, he was irritated and his eyes felt grainy and burning. He did not consider this to have been one of his better days.

"I know how you feel about Saladin. Hell, I feel the same way. I also know that no town marshal is gonna worry too awful much about some mule being slaughtered. Am I right?"

"There's no town marshal. I talked to the county sheriff. But you're right, of course. He wasn't much impressed by the crime."

"Exactly. Didn't figure he would be. But I know, and you know too if you bother to think about it, that there isn't much happens that somebody somewhere doesn't see or hear about or suspect. So I thought I'd ask around. You know?"

"Ask who?"

"The servants. The back alley folk. The cleaning women and stable boys and like that."

Dex began to get interested. He sat up straighter and quit thinking about his own discomforts of the moment. "Go on."

"Yeah, well, you and I both know that Sunday is the day off for most hired help, right? An' we both of us know that pretty much everywhere you go there's going to be a Sunday afternoon gathering place for the shadow folk."

"Shadow?" Dex asked.

"You know. The folk that're so unimportant that we aren't even seen. Mostly us blacks. Dex, you can walk down the street and folks will tip their hats and then behind your back they'll comment and pass judgment on how you're dressed and if you're walking straight or if you snubbed someone who passed by. Anyplace you go you'll be noticed and remarked on. People will remember. But me or any black man like me, we walk down the street and nobody even sees that we're there. I can knuckle my forelock and jump out of the path of a white lady on the sidewalk and bow and scrape till my head touches the ground. She won't once look at me. You could ask her five seconds later and she wouldn't be able to pick me out from a crowd of niggers even if all the rest of them were women. She wouldn't even notice that much. That's why I say we're shadow people, Dex. We might not even be there for all we're seen."

"I guess I hadn't particularly thought about that, but all right. Even saying it's so, what of it?"

"You white folks don't have any idea how much us shadow people see and hear, Dexter. You . . . and I'm not saying you in particular now but white folks in general . . . you pay so little attention that you'll do things in plain sight of us blacks that you'd be embarrassed as hell to admit to a white, never mind being seen doing these things. Not by anyone who counts, you wouldn't."

"Go on."

"So like I was saying, I figured there had to be some

place where I could go and make the acquaintance of some of the shadow folk here in Benson.''

"I take it you found such a place?''

"Of course I did. There's a grove of trees out east of town. The people gather there on their days off. Drink a little homemade whiskey. Roll some bones. Have a cock fight sometimes. You know.''

Dex nodded.

While he spoke James was stripping off his clothing, hanging each item meticulously on a peg, preparing for bed. He sat on the side of his cot and leaned forward so he could see around the front of the wardrobe while he talked with Dex.

"I drank a little and bought a lot, Dex. Lost some of our money wagering on the dice, too. I counted it as an investment though.''

"What'd you learn, James?''

"Nobody saw Saladin being killed. Not exactly. I mean there wasn't any actual eyewitness to the slaughter. But about eleven, maybe eleven thirty last night there was a fellow who called on that Charles Reggoner that was so mad about losing money to us yesterday.''

"You know I figure he's the one wanted to get back at us. But who is this second man and what would he have to do with it?''

"I never heard of him myself. Maybe you know him. The houseboy I talked to said he's somebody called Melon. Or something like that. This boy was pretty drunk by the time we got to talking. Do you know anybody with a name like that?''

Dex had to think for a minute. "I met a George Mullen. He's partners with Tyler Whitcomb at the bank. Could that be him?''

"It sounds close, but I couldn't say that for sure. Maybe there's somebody around with the nickname Melon. I doubt it though. This nigger boy I talked to wasn't the sort to use a white man's nickname. He's learned the hard way to be respectful and keep his head down. You know?''

Dex grunted. He knew. True respect is something that

has to be earned. But there is a feigned variety of it that can be enforced by way of intimidation. Yeah, he knew what James meant by that all right.

"Did this man say Melon had something to do with killing Saladin then?"

"Not exactly. All he knows for sure is that this Melon, or Mullen or whoever, came calling on your friend Reggoner late last night. The two of them talked for just a little while inside Regonner's house and then Reggoner got his hat and coat and the two white men went somewhere. They didn't walk out in the street in plain sight, either. My new friend said they went around back to the alley and went through it in the direction of town. Toward this hotel, in other words. He said they acted strange when they left, walking like they didn't want anybody to see them. He said he's never known Reggoner to do anything like that before and never known Melon to come to Reggoner's house so late. Said Melon comes to visit pretty often . . . I gather the two of them are related somehow though he didn't explain what the relationship is . . . but Melon has never come in the middle of the night like that before, and he's never seen Reggoner set foot in that alley until last night, much less take it when he went out to walk someplace."

"But he didn't know where they went or what they did there?"

James shook his head. "He only knew what I already told you. He couldn't say for sure about anything else."

"Was Reggoner . . . I don't know . . . were his clothes bloody when he came home? Anything like that?"

"I asked, but he said he wasn't up to know what time Reggoner got back or if he acted funny. My man said he went to bed a few minutes after Reggoner left the house. Figured he wouldn't be called on for anything more that night if the bossman was out tomcatting around or something, so he went on to bed himself."

"Reggoner goes out tomcatting much, does he?"

"Never. Not unless last night was the first time. I did think to ask that, too," James said.

Dex mulled over the news. It certainly was not conclusive. Not of anything more than a stroll in the moonlight. Still, it was damned well suspicious. "Would this man talk to me about it? Maybe I could, I don't know, maybe I could think of different ways to approach the questions, get him to remember more than he thinks he does."

"Oh, I could bring him by to meet with you someplace, Dex. Not here, of course. Not in plain sight. But I could get you and him together. 'Course I know what he'd say. 'No suh, mastuh suh, I didn't see nawthin', suh; that nigger James he tryin' to get ol' Rastus in trouble, suh, don' you b'lieve him, suh, I didn't see not nawthin' that night, no suh.' And that's about all you'd get out of him."

Dex wrinkled his nose. "Somebody named the poor son of a bitch Rastus? Really?"

"Jeez, Dex. Grow up. Of course he isn't really named Rastus. I was trying to make a point, that's all. His name is Barnabus. If it matters, which it doesn't."

"Oh. Sorry." Dex sighed. "One thing's for sure, James. You accomplished a hell of a lot more today than I did."

"You got Saladin's carcass removed though. At least you did that much."

"How'd you know that?"

"I spent half the evening with the man who dragged him off."

"Really? I never saw him. Didn't want to watch, actually. I talked to the people downstairs about it. Paid three dollars to have Saladin hauled off and buried."

James made a face. "The hotel manager charged John Shiver fifty cents for him to buy the carcass."

"What?"

"I kinda thought you wouldn't know anything about that. Which is why I brought it up. I just wanted you to know, I suppose. Shiver was there this evening. He's a high yella nigger. A farmer. He raises hogs, chickens, table vegetables. He wanted the meat to add to the feed for his sows and said he'll grind some up for the hens too. He'll keep the hide and tan it. There won't be anything go to waste."

"Dammit, I wanted that mule buried decent. He earned that much."

"No, Dex, it's just a dead mule. No reason John's chickens and hogs shouldn't benefit or that he shouldn't get some leather out of the deal."

"But that sonuvabitch downstairs charged both me and your friend Shiver."

"Sure he did. And both of you got what you wanted out of the deal. Leave it be, Dex. We got worse things than that to think about. Like getting some sleep for one thing."

Dex wasn't happy about that news. But he wasn't angry with James any longer either. "Go to sleep, James. Maybe things will look better in the morning."

"Maybe they will," James said. He did not sound like he particularly believed that.

"Good night."

"G'night your own self."

Dex blew the lamp out and lay down. He was asleep within seconds.

· 21 ·

Dex was careful on Monday morning to take his time about dressing and calling at the bank to claim his winnings from Charles Reggoner. He did not want to appear overly eager for the money. All the more so because of his suspicion—certainty was more like it—that Reggoner was the cowardly son of a bitch who either killed Saladin himself or arranged for someone else to do it for him. Damn the man!

It would not do, though, to show anger or point fingers. Proof in a court of law was not at all what Dex had in mind here. His visit yesterday with Sheriff Mickens showed clearer than words could have the sort of result he would obtain even if he had proof enough to take the matter to court. A half-hearted scolding and a ten-dollar fine would be the worst punishment Benson's law would likely impose. That would be the most that Dex could hope for here. And the dismissal of a stranger's charges would be far more probable.

Dex wanted Reggoner to pay for what he'd done. Genuinely pay. What Dex thirsted for now was not jurisprudence but retribution on a deep and personal level.

He fully intended to have it.

Toward that end he steeled himself against public displays of wrath or indignation and dressed himself with care.

The primary departure from his normal attire was that, everything considered, he no longer felt comfortable ambling about through this community with nothing in the way of personal protections save charm and a smile.

With that in mind, and given his new assessment of Charles Reggoner's character, Dexter unpacked his pair of soft leather shoulder holsters and the slim, light but lethal little .32 caliber revolvers that he rather rarely bothered to wear. Today and for the balance of their stay in Benson, though, he intended to have his guns ready to hand. Just in case.

He also determined that from now on it would be prudent for him to carry a cane. His cane in particular. The gentleman's accessory in question had a stout and sturdy looking Malacca shaft and a brass eagle's-beak head. That much was quite readily seen. What was not so apparent was that inside the hollowed out Malacca resided a sword blade of highest quality Toledo steel. A twist of Dex's wrist released the sword and allowed its withdrawal from the cane body. And Dexter Yancey was, if he did say so himself, a fencer of formidable skill. So, for that matter, was James. It was he, after all, against whom Dex had practiced since they both were children, and both of them had developed skills far beyond those of the average gentleman.

For the remainder of their stay in Benson, Dex had concluded while he pondered how they might approach this unpleasant business with Reggoner, he intended to keep himself armed, although without being obvious about it.

As for James, it would have been asking for trouble if James were to carry a pistol or sword. But it would be quite unremarkable for a black man to carry a pocket knife for utilitarian purposes. Among James's tasks today would be for him to find and acquire the largest lock-blade folding knife available here.

And in the meantime Dex would set about learning more about the quarry the two of them intended to pursue with all the diligence and considered malice of the Hounds of Hell.

◆ 22 ◆

Tyler Whitcomb was with someone when Dex arrived at the bank, so Dex idled about in the tiny lobby area. Until he realized that the presence of a stranger, even a well-dressed one, was making the teller nervous. The poor man began to sweat and fidget and kept sneaking sideways glances past the bars of his counter cage toward this unknown person, who hadn't stated any proper reason for being there.

After a few minutes of this Dex realized what the problem was. The teller undoubtedly suspected that Dexter was a hold-up artist awaiting the right combination of nerve and timing to pull out his guns and order everyone in the place to stand and deliver.

Dex resolved the fellow's worries by ambling over to him with a disarming smile. He nodded toward the glass window that separated Whitcomb's office from the working area of the bank. "I'm here to see Mr. Whitcomb," he explained. "He's expecting me."

The teller, a balding fellow in his forties or thereabouts, appeared visibly relieved. "I see." The man was even able now to return Dex's smile. "He won't be long, I'm sure. Would you like to sit while you're waiting, sir?"

"No, thank you." It occurred to Dexter that if indeed he had been a robber instead of a gentleman, this little bank would provide easy pickings. The teller didn't know him from Adam's off ox but was quite willing to accept Dex's statements at face value. Moreover, he was willing to take Dexter inside the closed and presumably locked door to the area behind the counter and cages while he waited.

There were no chairs in the small lobby, only behind the tall oak divider, and the teller offered one for Dex's use. So obviously he was willing to allow Dex to enter the work area where the door of a large wall safe stood open to disclose shelves and shining steel drawer fronts, compartments that presumably would be stuffed with cash and securities.

Robbery would have been easy, but the truth was that Dex wasn't remotely tempted. Couldn't help but notice how easy it would be to turn robber, of course. But . . . it simply was not his style. After all, robbery is such a common, low-class thing, the sort of activity any fool might accomplish.

And Dexter did have his pride, after all. Besides, if he were ever going to rob someone it would have to be someone like Charles Reggoner. Someone who *deserved* to be robbed. Damn him.

Dex seethed every time he thought about poor, faithful, gallant Saladin whose great competitor's heart had been so cruelly stopped. He seethed all the more when he thought about Reggoner.

He wished, and not for the first time during this past day and night, that Tyler hadn't stepped in back at the race grounds to pour oil on the waters and stop the rush of emotions leading inexorably toward a duel. Dex would have loved to face Charles Reggoner head-on.

He'd been the aggrieved party. The choice of weapons would have been his, and he knew exactly what he would have selected. Steel. He was sure he could best a pompous welsher like Reggoner with sword or pistol either one, but it was the sword he would have chosen. He wondered idly if Reggoner even would have had the nerve to show up for the contest.

Failure to do so would surely have ruined him. It would have exposed him for a coward. Well, in Louisiana such a thing would ruin a man. It would be regarded as proof that he was no gentleman, and no man of good repute nor woman of decent character would associate with him. Here in Texas, Dex could only assume that it would have been the same.

He was viewing in his mind's eye a combat—to the death? he hadn't gotten quite that far in his imagination yet—when the bank teller cleared his throat and softly said, "Sir? Sir? Mr. Whitcomb is free now."

Dex hadn't noticed the other customer, a man roughly dressed in a farmer's overalls and a freshly boiled and starched shirt deemed suitable among that sort for formal wear, conclude his business and leave the bank. Now that his attention was drawn to the fact, however, he saw that Tyler's door was open and the office empty save for the bank owner.

"Who shall I say is calling, sir?" the teller asked.

Dex told him and was quickly ushered inside the office.

· 23 ·

"What a terrible shame, Mr. Yancey, terrible."

"Please call me Dexter."

"Of course, but I do hope you will accept my sympathy and my apologies. Something like that," Whitcomb shook his head, "reflects on our entire community. Youngsters, I should think. Disreputable sorts. We ... everyone ... has those from time to time. The pity is that it should involve you and that wonderful animal of yours. Really I was looking forward to a rematch."

"Yes, sir, so was I," Dex said.

"I hope you'll not think ill of us because of it."

"No, sir, I couldn't possibly do that. You, after all, have been more than kind."

"Yes, well, um, not so kind as I would like to be. I did speak with Dan Mickens yesterday afternoon. He believes as I do that rowdy youngsters are at fault, but in truth, Dexter, he tells me there is very little likelihood that they will be caught. If they are," Whitcomb spread his hands, "boys of that ilk are almost certain to come from the lower order. Negroes, Mexicans, I'm sure you understand what I mean."

"Yes, sir, I do."

"Even if they were found it is unlikely that you could recover. Certainly you would never recoup the true value of a fine animal like that. The best you could hope for would be an award of a pittance."

"I understand that, of course," Dex told him.

"I did make it clear to Dan that his fullest efforts are desired in this matter," Whitcomb said.

"Thank you, sir."

"I've also had a small word with Henry Adams."

"I don't believe I know Mr. Adams," Dex said.

"Henry runs the livery in town. Buys and sells livestock. If you and your manservant intend to travel on by horseback you will be dealing with Henry. I've let him know I would consider it a personal favor if he were to, ahem, treat you with consideration."

"That's mighty kind of you, sir."

"The least I could do, my young friend, after the way you've been received in Benson." He smiled. "At least you'll not leave empty handed, eh?"

Whitcomb reached for a brass bell but paused when Dex said, "Oh, I'll not be leaving Benson just yet."

"No?"

"No, sir. I have some business to conclude here first."

"I see. That is very good news indeed, Dexter." Whitcomb's expression did not entirely match his words. The "good news" statement was not at all reflected in his facial expression or in his posture. If anything, Dex thought, the courtly banker looked a bit put out at the idea that Dex intended to remain in Benson.

"Is there, um, is there anything I can help you with, Dexter? About this, uh, business, that is?"

"No, sir, and if you don't mind I'll not go into specifics about the prospects I envision here." Dex did not offer particulars for the very good reason that he could not. He had no idea what excuse he would use to remain. But remain he most certainly would. Sheriff Mickens might have no interest in apprehending Saladin's killer. Dex himself did not take the matter so lightly. It would, however, have been foolish to say anything of that to Tyler Whitcomb, no matter how decent and helpful the gentleman wished to be.

"Of course, sir. No offense taken, I assure you." Whitcomb's smile was thin and not entirely convincing. "I assume you do want to collect your winnings from Saturday, do you not?"

"I do indeed, sir." And that was certainly the truth. The take from Saturday would be the last income poor Saladin would provide for them. From here on Dex and James would have to think of some other way to make their way. Until now, with Saladin to count on, it had all seemed quite simple. Make a match, lay a wager, collect the winnings. From here on making a livelihood might not prove to be quite so easy.

Again, however, that was not something he wanted to discuss with Tyler Whitcomb.

"This will only take a moment, Dexter." Whitcomb rang the small bell, and a moment later the bank's cashier came in response. "Bring me five hundred in cash, please, John." He looked at Dex. "Do you prefer currency or coin?"

"Currency if it's convenient."

Whitcomb nodded and said to his cashier, "If you please, John. And debit the amount to Charles Reggoner."

The cashier looked acutely uncomfortable at the instruction. He looked from Whitcomb to Dexter and back again. After several moments of apparent indecision he walked rather stiffly around behind Tyler Whitcomb's desk and bent down so he could whisper into the gentleman's ear.

Whitcomb listened in silence. Then frowned. "You can't . . ." He clamped his mouth shut in a thin, firm line. "Just bring the five hundred, John," he said. "Take it from my account for the moment."

The clerk stood upright and would have left, but Dex stopped him with a gesture and a scowl. "I have no idea what the problem is, Tyler, but you owe me nothing. I'll not accept money drawn against your account, sir. If I am reading this situation correctly, I will not only expect my winnings be taken from Reggoner's accounts, I believe I shall insist, sir, that they be delivered from his hand. His own hand and no other."

"I . . . I can't believe that any of this is happening, Dexter. Truly I am embarrassed and appalled."

"Yes, sir. May I assume Mr. Reggoner was here earlier today in order to strip his cash accounts?"

"I . . . you know I cannot comment about any of my depositors, Dexter. That would not be ethical."

"No, sir. But I think I've come to know you well enough to realize that you'd not countenance anything that would be less than . . . gentlemanly."

Whitcomb shook his head. And said nothing. The silence, of course, said volumes.

Dex stood. He extended his hand to Whitcomb with a half bow. "Thank you for your courtesies, sir. You are a gentleman." He nodded abruptly to the bank clerk, spun on his heels and left the building.

• 24 •

"Why, that son of a bitch," James grumbled.

"This is not exactly a big surprise. The man is no gentleman."

James grinned. "Isn't that what he said about you?"

"Yeah," Dex agreed. "But he was wrong. I'm not."

"Self-confident this morning, aren't you?"

"Only when I'm sure of the ground I'm standing on."

"Like I said . . ." James added with a smile.

"After lunch," Dex said, changing the subject, "I'm going to go down to the livery stable. We need another horse anyway, and I want to ask the man there about this Reggoner fellow." Dex grinned. "Tyler Whitcomb was nice enough to tell the man at the livery that he should be cooperative with me. What I'm thinking is that the gentleman didn't think to say anything about limiting that cooperation just to the selling of horses. Do you want to come along?"

James shook his head. "I couldn't add anything to the conversation anyhow. He'd think it strange if you let a black man join in, even though I *am* smarter than you and better looking, too. No, you go on alone. I'll poke around on my own and see what I can find out."

"Do you want lunch downstairs then?"

James made a face. "The food is terrible here."

"It's pretty good in the restaurant."

"That may be, but the stuff they serve at the back step tastes like shit."

"Forage for yourself then if you can do any better that way."

James's teeth flashed starkly white against the milk chocolate hue of his skin. "Doesn't much matter if this one can cook good or not. She has other attributes to recommend her."

"Not the same little gal with the big tits that disappointed you the other night," Dex said.

"Oh, no. I had enough of that one. This is a new girl. Spotted her yesterday."

Dex shook his head. But he didn't say anything. He couldn't. He was in no position to point fingers when it came to a wandering eye and an appreciation of nearly anything in a skirt. He settled for asking, "Is there anything you want me to look for when I dicker for a horse?"

"Yeah," James told him. "Find us one that's faster than Saladin was."

"That will be the day, won't it."

James sighed. "You're lucky if you come across one animal like that in a lifetime. And that's only if you've been living right."

"I think what it comes down to is that you and I are out of the horse racing business."

"If we have to, dammit," James declared, "we'll just send you out to take a job and support us."

"Why me?" Dex asked.

James gave him an innocent look. "They ain't gonna hire no po' ol' black boy at high wage, bawss. Gotta be you."

Dex was chuckling when he went downstairs to inquire about the lunch menu.

• 25 •

Henry Adams, the livery keeper, was a leathery man with steel-gray hair, watery eyes and a runny nose that he dabbed at frequently with a kerchief that looked like it hadn't been washed since Henry left grade school.

"Oh, yes," Adams said when Dex introduced himself. "Mr. Whitcomb said I should expect you. Said you're a friend of his and he expects me to treat you right. I'd do that anyway, o' course."

"Yes, sir, I'm sure you would," Dex said agreeably. After all, it was well known that virtually all horse traders were honest and honorable men who had only the best interests of their customers in mind. Right.

"I got a few decent horses you can choose from. Out back here if you wanta come this way, Mr. Yancey. Right back . . . par'n me?"

"I want to see them, of course, but could we sit down in private and have a little talk first please, Mr. Adams?"

Adams blinked, used the blue-white- and snot-colored kerchief to wipe his nose again, then nodded. "If you like, sure. We'll go in my office there."

The "office" was the feed and tack room, although a tiny writing desk, the sort of lightweight thing an army officer might take with him in the field, was tucked into one corner, and there were several upended nail kegs placed around to act as stools. The desk was cluttered with scraps of paper. The walls were just as littered, hung with saddles, harnesses, snaffle bits, hobbles, quirts and unidentifiable straps and buckles. The place smelled of leather and saddle soap. Dex found the odors of the tack room homey and in truth rather pleasant.

"Set there, son." Adams pointed to a keg that once had held horseshoe nails and chose himself to sit beside his "office" table. He crossed his legs and patiently waited for Dex to state his business.

Dexter took the seat indicated but before launching into any questions pulled a flat pint bottle from the side pocket of his coat. "I thought you might join me in a little nip first," he suggested, offering the bottle to Henry Adams. "I stopped by the store on my way over just now. This is the best they had available."

Adams laughed and said, "Son, I told you already that Mr. Whitcomb asked me to do right by you, and so I shall. You don't need to soften me up none or try an' get me pie-eyed a'forehand."

"Oh, it wasn't that, sir. Mr. Whitcomb said I could trust you for a fair deal on the horse. I was just trying to be sociable, that's all." Which was only half a lie. Dexter truly didn't much give a damn about the horse dealing. After all, a horse is only a means to get from here to there. This business with Charles Reggoner, though . . . that was a matter of honor. And that Dex was taking very seriously indeed.

So while he really did not intend to get Adams drunk in the hope of striking a better price on a horse, he did hope to loosen the fellow's tongue about certain of his fellow townsfolk.

"I understand that, son, and I'm sure it's so," Adams said, indicating as clearly as if he'd posted it on a chalkboard for passersby to read that he did not believe a word Dex was telling him. "Fact is though that I'm a teetotaler. Took the temperance pledge," he pursed his lips, rolled his eyes and swiped the kerchief under his nose again, "eighteen and sixty three, it would have been. Bunch of us boys raiding with Stuart found a root cellar with a couple kegs of scuppernong wine in it. Sweetest, smoothest, slickest tasting stuff I ever put in my mouth, let me tell you. Me and the rest of the boys in the squadron took to drinking that wine, and they tell me that I lost a couple days afterward. Next thing I remember we was in the middle of the damnedest battle I ever did see. At a place name of Gettysburg. Maybe you've heard of it."

"I expect that I have, yes sir."

Adams shook his head and wiped his nose. "Scared me plumb spitless, I don't mind telling you. I swore off the grape right then and there and haven't had a drop since."

Dex grinned. "This stuff is grain not grape, if that makes a difference, sir."

Adams laughed. "You aren't half bad, son, but I'm not interested. Put your bottle away. But don't you worry. I don't hold it against you that you tried. Might have done the same myself once. Now then . . . just what is it that you're wanting to talk about in here where we can't be overheard. I got to think that it isn't one of my horses that you're here to talk about just now, else we'd be out back at least a'looking them over first."

The old boy wasn't stupid, that was for sure, Dex acknowledged.

Which might very well turn out to be of benefit if he proved willing to open up and discuss local affairs with a properly recommended stranger.

"Well, sir," Dex said, "it's kind of like this. . . ."

· 26 ·

"I was at the races this weekend past," Dex told the livery owner.

"Yes, I heard something about that," Adams said, quiet amusement wrinkling the corners of his eyes. Very likely the entire community for some miles around had heard considerable about the weekend's entertainments.

"And I happened to, well, to notice a young lady who was in attendance there." Dex had thought long and hard about how he should approach the man in his quest for information. And while very few men—gentleman or otherwise—are inclined to gossip about their neighbors, practically no one can resist the lure of matchmaking and romantic intrigues. Dex was hoping that Henry Adams was no exception to that norm.

"Go on," Adams prompted when Dex quite deliberately hesitated so as to be able to gauge the man's willingness to pursue the subject.

"Yes, well, I was not the only gentleman to take an interest in her. And I, uh, frankly, sir, I was curious about both of them."

"And they would be?"

"The gentleman in question is a Mr. Charles Reggoner."

Something—Dex was not at all sure what—flickered across Adams's expression but was hidden too quickly to be read with any degree of certainty. "Your question is in regard to a girl, you said?"

"There was also the matter of a wager, as you may well have heard," Dex admitted.

"Damn near came to a duel is the way I heard it."

Adams sounded about halfway disappointed that there had been no fight, so Dex risked the comment, "Not yet, sir."

Adams grunted but said nothing.

"I, um, could not help noticing before that, sir, that Mr. Reggoner was paying particular attention to a most attractive young woman, you see."

"Was he now. And she would be . . . ?"

"We were not introduced, you see, so I can't give you her name," Dex said. "But I believe she would be the daughter of Mr. Whitcomb's partner, George Mullen."

Adams frowned. "You are mistaken about that, Mr. Yancey."

"Are you quite sure?"

"No doubt 'bout it. Mullen has no daughters. Has a son by his first wife. The boy is away at school. But nope, no daughters. None."

It was Dex's turn to frown. "I certainly thought . . . she is very pretty, as I said. Fair complexion. Red hair. About . . . did I say something odd, sir? The look you're giving me suggests that I did."

"Red hair, you say. And young Reggoner was in her company often. Aye, he would be. They're brother and sister."

Dex frowned again, more deeply this time. "I don't believe I understand. Charles Reggoner is most assuredly not the son of Mr. Mullen. Yet you say Reggoner and this young woman are brother and sister."

"Oh, it's simple enough, young man," Adams assured him. "The young lady is Mullen's wife. Amanda Mullen now. Used t' be Amanda Reggoner. An' Charles of course is Mullen's brother-in-law."

"I didn't guess any of that." But it did, Dex realized, fit very snugly with the information James had gotten from Reggoner's houseboy. The caller late Saturday night would indeed have been George Mullen, and the two men were related by marriage just as the houseboy had suggested.

"Didn't come here t' ask me about Amanda Mullen neither," Adams said with a wry twitch of his lip that might have been a smile stillborn.

"No?"

"No," Adams said with no room for doubting in his tone of voice. "I was out there Saturday, Mr. Yancey. You wouldn't't've noticed, but your man would remember me. I'm always invited. Do the shoeing if there's any needs done. I had my forge set up out by the picket line. Saw most of the exchange between you and Charles and heard plenty more about it afterward. Heard too that he said later he'd be damned if he'd pay what he owes you. Truth is, I don't countenance a man not paying his debts. And that was one fine mule you had there. It was a pleasure to see him run, and it hurt me deep to hear somebody was cruel enough to destroy a magnificent animal like that one. Which I will tell you straight out is the reason I don't mind you coming to me today with some cockamamie story about you being interested in another man's missus."

Dex reminded himself to not take this lanky and unimpressive-appearing livery man lightly again in the future. Adams was sharper than he seemed.

"What you really want t' know is about Charles, isn't it?"

"I, uh, I am more than a mite curious, yes sir."

"I will tell you outright, Mr. Yancey. I know Charles. Knew his father before him and most of the family. They act right grand, the Reggoners do, but it's all for show. Not the sort of folk you want to turn your back on. An' if it comes to a duel between you and Charles, Mr. Yancey, I hope you are both quick and accurate with your guns, because he sure as hell will be. They say Charles has killed two men in arguments over cards."

"The other gentlemen won and pressed for payment, I would presume."

"I wouldn't know anything about that," Adams said. "The little I know is only hearsay. Folks claim he's gotten himself into scrapes before somewhere over around Austin, but I can't say for sure about any of it. It's just what I hear. My advice to you though, Mr. Yancey, is to avoid fighting with him. He's fast with a gun when he needs t' be, and he won't miss."

Fast with a gun. It was an expression Dex had heard often enough, but it was not a subject he knew much about. Speed of action had nothing to do with the deliberate accuracy he'd been taught. But then Dex's education had to do not with gunfights as they might be undertaken here in Texas where revolving cylinder six-shooters held sway but with performance on a field of honor. Dexter's own expertise lay with the handsomely crafted if slightly archaic single shot, muzzle-loaded dueling pistol.

He owned a pair of light revolvers, true, and in fact was wearing them even as he spoke with Adams. But he had never given thought to jerking them out of their holsters with any great urgency such as Adams suggested Reggoner would do.

That indeed was a warning Dex would have to keep in mind if—when—he had further dealings with Reggoner.

"I appreciate your kindness in telling me this, Mr. Adams," Dex said. He meant that quite sincerely.

Adams only shrugged. "Mr. Whitcomb said I was t' take care of you the best I could. I figure this part of it is more important than whatever you and me do when it comes to horse dealing."

"Yes sir, I believe you may well be right about that."

"Do you want t' buy another horse, Mr. Yancey?"

"Yes, I do."

"Need one real soon, do you?" There was that look of partially concealed amusement in the man's eyes again.

"Not so awful soon," Dex admitted.

"I didn't think so. Tell you what. You seem a nice enough young fellow, and Mr. Whitcomb wants you looked after. I won't show you anything that I got in my pen right now. Give me a couple days to look around. Mayhap I can find something that I'd like to see you astride. Maybe even a couple horses, good ones, that you'd be willing to trade your present horse against. Straight up trade, and I give you my own personal guarantee that the two you get will be good ones.''

''I would take your word and gladly, Mr. Adams,'' Dex said, ''but I will confess that you do have my curiosity aroused now. Why ever would you propose such a thing as that?''

Adams laughed. ''Because when he told me he wanted you treated right, Mr. Yancey, he also told me that he wants me t' buy your horse for him. It's Mr. Whitcomb wants the animal, not me. Personally I wouldn't have him. Don't get me wrong. He's pretty. Any fool can see that. But if I know anything at all about horses, sir, and I like t' think that I do, that horse will run slow as a hog in deep mud. He doesn't have the chest or the windpipe to hold any speed for more than a furlong or two.'' Adams wiped his nose with the kerchief and added, ''Only fair t' tell you that I've explained all this to Mr. Whitcomb already. An' he told me in turn that there's a particular reason why he wants that horse of your'n and that you yourself already confessed it to him that the horse is not a runner. Truth is, that had a lot t' do with why I'm willing to talk plain to you now. Means you're an honest man, Mr. Yancey. I admire that, and if I was still a drinking man I would've been proud to drink with you. I want you should know that, sir.''

''I consider that a high compliment, Mr. Adams, and I thank you for your candor.''

''Candor.'' Adams repeated the word as if he were tasting it. ''That's kind've like honesty, right?''

''Yes, sir.''

Adams nodded, then wiped his nose. ''Candor. Yes, I like that. Do I have your permission to look for a pair of animals t' trade on Mr. Whitcomb's behalf then?''

''You do, sir, and I will be pleased to accept your judgment as to a fair replacement.''

Adams chuckled. "My judgment, Mr. Yancey, would've been to offer you two, maybe three dollars cash money for your horse. But I'll do what Mr. Whitcomb wants, and you should be pleased enough when you an' your man decide t' leave here. You'll be mounted decent, I can promise you that."

Dex stood and offered his hand to the man. "Believe me, Mr. Adams, it has been a pleasure visiting with you this afternoon. And about the new horses . . . I won't be needing them any time soon."

"No, I sort've expected maybe you wouldn't," Adams said.

Dex headed back to the hotel, hoping to find James there. He wanted to mull over his newfound knowledge and hear what James had to say about Reggoner and George Mullen and the relationship between the two of them.

But what a terrible pity, really, that Amanda Mullen was married. Such a waste.

He smiled.

Or then again perhaps not.

• 27 •

It was past nine o'clock in the evening before James returned to the hotel room. Dex greeted him eagerly and was quick to spill the things he'd learned that afternoon from Henry Adams.

"Did you find out anything more?" Dex asked when he was done with his own spiel.

"Plenty," James said. "The same things you did about the sister, of course, and that fellow Mullen, who pretty much has to be the man Barnabus was talking about when I thought he was saying *Melon*. All of that fits together tidy as a picture puzzle.

"The person I was talking to didn't say anything about your friend Reggoner being good with a gun. I don't think she's the sort to know or care very much about guns anyway."

"She?" Dex teased with a grin.

"Don't get jealous. This wasn't the girl I expected to be with. In fact, I never got around to seeing her today. Instead I talked with a couple men who work around town, and one of them told me about this woman I should see. So I went over and called on her, and I'm glad I did.

"Her name is Emma. She's in her forties, I think, but

she looks older. She's had a rough time of things. Has a couple woods-colt boys who give her grief. She spent a lot of time talking about them. Not that I wanted to hear it, mind, but I think she doesn't get to talk very much. Or maybe it's that she doesn't want to air her own family's dirty linen with folks she knows, but she felt a little freer about speaking with a stranger who's just passing through. Anyway, when she did get off the subject of her boys and talked about Reggoner she had a lot to say. None of it was good, I can tell you that.

"Emma used to work for Reggoner's family. Belonged to them when she was younger, then stayed on and worked for them." James grinned. "Kind of like somebody else I can think of in this room right now."

"You're just damn lucky it's against the law nowadays or I'd have you strung up and whipped now and then, just to hold your attention," Dex blustered.

"Your daddy did do that a couple times that I can remember, you know," James said softly. "Not to me, of course, but I saw it done, Dex. Twice, I think. I don't expect I'll ever forget the sound that snake made when it hit flesh."

Dex felt his cheeks begin to burn. "I'm sorry, James. I didn't mean . . ."

"I know you didn't. You were joking around. It's just . . . not a joking subject for me. You know what I mean?"

"Yes. I'll try and not say shit like that again."

"Yeah, well, what I was saying, this Emma belonged to the Reggoner family. Then she worked for them a while until some time after Charles and Amanda's mother died. I gather that the father was a son of a bitch, too. She didn't exactly say so, but he might've been the father of her boys. She sort of hinted around at that. Bad blood in them, that sort of thing. The mother was all right. Emma liked her and stayed with the family until a few years ago when the mother died. Charles kept her on but reduced her pay. She'd been making four dollars a week, and he cut that in half."

"Two dollars a week," Dex said.

"That's right. And whatever food she could eat at the house. If she wanted to take anything home to her sons she had to sneak it out."

"I hope she took plenty."

"I'm sure she did," James said. "That would've been only fair, though I guess Charles would have had her charged if she'd been caught. Anyway, she stayed working there only until Amanda married Charles's close pal Mullen, then she quit. Now she takes in laundry, cleans houses and stores, whatever she can find. She says she makes out a lot better now than she did with the Reggoners. She said now she can earn five, sometimes as much as six dollars a week. She has a little house down along the creek that menfriends built for her. She'd get them to pitch in with some lumber or a few hours of work on it, whatever they could do. Fucked her way into having a home, I guess."

"You can't much blame her for that," Dex said.

"No, you sure can't."

"Anyway, back to Charles," Dex prompted. "One thing I want to know is what passions drive him? And what does he do for a living?"

"Right. Emma knows more than Charles or Mullen either one thinks she does. Like I've told you before, us niggers aren't but shadows. There's some whites who think we don't have feelings or ears or any intelligence at all, and they will say just the damnedest things in front of us."

Dex nodded. "I know."

"Charles and Mullen must be like that, because Emma overheard a lot of their talk when she worked in that house. She doesn't know what schemes they're up to now, of course, since she doesn't go there anymore. But this Mullen is an investor in Mr. Whitcomb's bank. He isn't actively involved in the bank. That is, he doesn't go to work or do anything in particular there. But apparently he has a financial stake in it. Maybe he invested when Whitcomb was starting the business or . . . I don't know. Emma doesn't know much about business affairs, so she was pretty hazy about that part of it. She does know that Mullen is in some kind of partnership with your Mr. Whitcomb.

"Mullen is also in partnership with Charles. But . . . and here's the interesting part . . . Tyler Whitcomb has no idea that Mullen is associated with Reggoner in a business way. He knows they're friends, of course. Everyone in town knows that and about the relationship by Mullen's marriage to Amanda. But Emma says the two are in some sort of deal to make money off farmers in the country around here."

"Do you know what sort of business that would be?" Dex asked.

James shook his head. "Emma says she doesn't understand what it is that the two of them do, exactly. She says she heard some of their talk about it but she didn't understand what it meant. She knows that George Mullen doesn't want Mr. Whitcomb to find out about it. She's sure about that. Mr. Whitcomb wouldn't approve. She also knows that it's Charles who handles most of this scheme, whatever it is. And then the two of them split the profits after."

Dex grunted. That was the sort of knowledge that might be useful. But they would have to find out more. "What about Saladin?" he asked. That, really, was the crux of his interest in Charles Reggoner. And in George Mullen, too, for that matter.

"Emma doesn't know. But she did say that both men are vindictive sons of bitches."

"She said that?"

"She didn't use the word 'vindictive,' if that's what you're asking. But she sure as hell did emphasize the terminology 'sons of bitches' when she spoke about them. She says that getting even by killing Saladin is the sort of thing that either one of them would do."

"Did you ask her what Reggoner and Mullen most care about?" Dex asked.

"Damn right I did. She said they both dote on money more than anything else. And Amanda. Mullen is crazy about Charles's little sister. He's as horny for her as a feist dog in a room full of bitches in season."

"And the girl?"

"She didn't want to marry the old goat. Emma says her brother forced her into it somehow, and she cried for two weeks solid before the wedding."

Dex fingered his chin and thought for a time. When he spoke again his voice was slow and contemplative. "We'll need to find out more about this scheme Reggoner and Mullen have to bilk money out of farmers. If it's something they don't want Tyler to know about then it's probably illegal and certainly unethical. Tyler wouldn't put up with either of those. So we need to learn exactly what it is that they do." Dex sat up straighter on the side of his bed and grinned. "Once we know what it is that we have to work with here, we'll have to see if we can't strip some of that money from the gentlemen . . . if I may so loosely use the word . . . and deposit it into our own coffers."

James patted his belly in the vicinity of the money belt that he wore hidden there. "Just see that our end of it has to do with coffers and not coffins, all right?"

"The risks, I promise you, will be all yours," Dex pledged.

"God, it's good to have friends," James said with a chuckle.

· 28 ·

The following morning Dex fortified himself with a hearty breakfast and had the hotel pack a lunch large enough for two before having poor, useless Galahad saddled and hiring a nag for James to ride.

Dex was curious about why Tyler Whitcomb would want to buy Galahad. But he didn't want to ruin any of the banker's plans, for a joke or a wager or whatever, by asking too many questions of the unusually perceptive livery owner. Tyler, he was sure, would have good reason for wanting the glacially slow animal. And Tyler was already very much aware of the horse's little trick when it came to the limping.

In any event, Henry Adams had not yet found a pair of horses that he liked for Dex and so they took Galahad out—the exercise would do him good after several days of standing about in a stall—as well as an exceptionally ugly little rat-tailed roan for James to use.

"This isn't quite the same as striding out on Saladin," James observed when they were out of the hearing of anyone else.

"No, I doubt either one of us will feel anything like that ever again," Dex agreed.

"Mind if I ask you something?" James said.

"Go ahead."

"D'you happen to have *any* idea where the hell we're going this morning?"

Dex grinned at him. "Not the foggiest. Your ladyfriend said she didn't know what farms Reggoner and Mullen were interested in, just that she knew it had something to do with farmers. Right?"

James nodded.

"So we're going to stop at a lot of farms today and ask to water our horses. Or something."

"I always like it when you have a clear-cut plan in mind, Dexter. Gives me confidence in you, it does."

Dex groaned. He felt bloated and bilious from all the fried pies, cornpone and clabber that had been damn near forced on them the whole day long. Every farm they stopped at welcomed them—well, welcomed Dex and were politely agreeable to James, who they assumed to be Dex's servant—with invitations to stay for the next meal and, barring that, an insistence that Dex partake of whatever marvel had just that moment, practically, come out of the oven.

By the time they turned the horses around and started back to Benson Dex was resenting the very idea of southern hospitality. His belly groaned from the intrusion of all those heavy foods, and the hotel's carefully packaged lunch hadn't yet been touched.

Worse, though, they had not learned a damn thing in exchange for all that discomfort.

"I say next time, Dex, you come right out and ask people about Charles Reggoner."

"I don't want to do that. Not unless it's our last resort. Whatever he's up to, I don't want him to know that we're interested in it. Or him. It has to be something rotten or they wouldn't be afraid for Tyler to know about it. That's enough right there to tell me we got to slip up on this quiet as a coon entering a hen house."

"*Rac*-coon, if you don't mind," James said with a straight face.

"Yeah, that kind too."

James wadded up a pillow and flung it at Dexter, which precipitated several minutes of silent scuffling.

When they settled down again, both of them puffing from the exertion but pleased by the release of spirit and energy, James's unfocused gaze drifted away in the general direction of the ceiling.

"What are you thinking about?" Dex asked.

"There's something been chewing on me half the day long. I dunno, maybe it's just me, but . . . how many different places did we stop at today? Seven? Eight?"

"Something like that, I suppose. Why?"

"Did you notice something unusual at every one of them?"

"Unusual how?" Dex asked.

James looked away again for a moment in contemplation. Then he said, "Not unusual in any one place by itself, but it really strikes me odd when it's all put together."

"I don't know what you mean."

"The new stuff."

"Come again?"

"New stuff. Farm equipment. Every single place we went up along that river road today, every farm we stopped at, they had new stuff sitting around. Disk harrows. Hay rakes. Gang plows."

"I never noticed."

"That's because you were so busy undressing all those white women in your mind."

"Only a few of them," Dex said in a wounded tone of voice. "Most of them were too ugly. But the daughter at that next to last place . . ." He rolled his eyes and whistled softly.

"No tits," James offered.

"It isn't the tit that feels so good."

"Everybody to his own taste. But pay attention now, dammit. Get your mind back on business. Like I was trying to say just now, every single place we stopped at had a bunch of new stuff sitting around. You could see that because of all the bright, clean paint still on everything. Farm equipment lasts damn near forever, Dex. And it's used hard. A year, two at the most and all you see is sun bleached wood and weathered rust on a wagon or a plow or whatever."

Dex nodded. "That's true enough."

"But all those places today . . . no, excuse me, all of them except one . . . they had new equipment sitting around. Now why would a thing like that come to be?"

"Some really fast talking salesman came through here last winter?" Dex guessed.

"Come on now, get serious. Think about it. All those men have been spending heavy on new equipment. Do you think it's a coincidence that they can all afford to buy that stuff, all of them at the same time?"

"And you're suggesting . . . ?"

"I'm not suggesting anything. Yet. But I think it's kinda interesting. Especially since we know your boy Reggoner and his brother in law Mullen are up to something that involves money or maybe banking, something on that order of things. I'm saying maybe we should think about what we saw today and do some more looking around. That's all."

Dex grunted, then nodded again. "It's a start. Maybe." With a groan he leaned down and struggled to get his right boot off, rested for a moment and then attacked the left.

"Time to get ready and go down to dinner," James said cheerfully.

Dex gave him a look of disgust. "Don't you even mention food to me again. Not before Thursday at the earliest."

James laughed and stood up. "You can lie around in here like a slug if you want to. Me, I'm going to step out on the town tonight."

"Just don't wake me when you come in." Dex lay back on his bed fully clothed and threw the crook of his arm over his eyes to block out the last of the late afternoon sunlight.

◆ 29 ◆

Dex smiled. Practically beamed with delight as he accepted a tin cup of buttermilk that was cold from the springhouse. "Thank you."

"Salt in that, mister? I always like a dash of salt in my buttermilk."

"No, this is fine just like it is." He smiled again. Drank deeply. Used the back of his hand to wipe the milky residue from his upper lip. "Ahhh."

"More?"

"No, thanks." He knew better now than to accept too much from the generosity displayed at any one farm. After all, the day could prove to be a long one and he still felt mildly bilious from yesterday's overindulgences. "You could give my man a little though if you wouldn't mind."

Dex glanced at James, who could do nothing but stand there and act politely respectful. And of course grateful for whatever scraps this white family might pass his way. Anything else would not only be questioned, it would be resented and could even lead to serious trouble. James was stuck in his Yowzuh Bawss role and had to stay there, like it or not.

The thing was, James despised buttermilk. Detested the

stuff. Dex enjoyed it thoroughly, but James had always considered it only slightly more palatable than fermented horse urine. Dex knew that. And James knew that he knew it.

Well, James shouldn't have been so loud when he came in during the wee hours of the morning. Buttermilk seemed a small enough price to pay for disrupting an innocent man's slumbers. Or so Dex believed. Someday, he thought, he would have to inquire further about that . . . if he could ever find an innocent man to ask about it.

He looked at James with a perfectly innocent expression anyway while the farmer's wife found a crudely carved and not too dirty wooden cup that she filled to overflowing with the cold buttermilk and handed to James. He accepted the loathsome liquid—to him, at least—with a bob of his head and a vacuous grin and a mumble that might have been a thank-you. Or might just as easily have been a threat indicating Dex would pay for this just as soon as the two of them were alone again.

Dex turned to the woman's husband, and as if in afterthought asked, "Pardon me, sir, if my question is too personal, but I've a cousin in the farm supply business back home in Louisiana."

"Yes?"

"He heard I would be traveling in Texas and asked me to look into prospects here. He offers excellent rates. Or so he assures me. Personally I wouldn't know a good price from a bad one. Don't know much about any sort of business really, but my relative seems to know his trade and he's an honest man. Would there be good opportunity here for a gentleman in that line?"

The farmer, a man named Means, grunted and shook his head. "Not around here, no."

"I do notice your spreader over there," Dex said. "Handsome."

"Newest model," the farmer said with pride. "See that bed? Hold a quarter ton, that will. And you can even adjust the rate of delivery. Just change over the gears, easy as pie."

"Imagine that," Dex said with a cluck of his tongue.

"Are you as satisfied with your dealer as you are with the machine, sir?"

The farmer preened and puffed just a mite. "That's the best part, you see. Fella from this county bought out the stock of a failed merchant somewhere. Then he passed the equipment along to his neighbors at cost. Now wasn't that a fine thing for him to do?"

"Gracious yes, I should certainly say so," Dex agreed.

"Damned cheap, really. It was a stroke of luck," the farmer went on. "Would have been foolish for a man to pass up a chance like that. Not even once in a lifetime chance, I'd say. Most men farm their whole lives and never find themselves set up so nicely."

"It sounds like you were wise, sir. And a lucky thing you were able to take advantage of the opportunity when it presented itself."

"Margaret, go see to dinner. This gentleman will be staying to eat."

"Oh, thank you, sir, but I only stopped hoping to get a swallow of water. I couldn't impose further."

"No imposition at all, son. It's a pleasure to have guests and all the more so to have a fine gentleman such as yourself honor us by joining us at table. And my Margaret is a fine cook. Don't you ever doubt that, mister."

Dex smiled again—he'd been doing it so much the past couple days that his jaws hurt—and, doffing his hat, gave Margaret a slight bow. "Such doubt would never cross my mind, sir."

Means seemed as pleased as if he himself had been complimented.

"You were saying something about your new farm equipment?" Dex prompted although in fact Means had been done with the subject.

"Oh, yes. My new spreader. Not the only thing I bought from the gentleman either. Got a fine two-row plow as well. And for half what I would have expected to pay. This gentleman, local fellow from Benson just down the road there, this gentleman—I'd mention his name but he's very modest and asked me not to, besides it could be that he wasn't able to make this offer to just everyone and I wouldn't want to make any of my neighbors feel left out, you see—this gentleman not only gave me the equipment at cost, with no profit to himself, he arranged with a gentleman friend of his that I can pay for the machinery over time. Have you ever heard of such a generous thing as that?'' Means enthused.

"No," Dex said quite honestly, "I don't expect that I ever did."

"Well, it's true. Arranged for me to borrow the money from a friend of his. And at no interest, too. None. Just pay the amount back and that will be the end of it."

"Marvelous," Dex said.

"Tell your nigger to take himself and the horses into the shade over there, sir. I'll have one of my boys run some 'pone and clabber out to him while you join us for dinner."

"Oh, I do thank you, Mr. Means, and I hope you will repeat that invitation the next time I stop by. It will be a pleasure to share your company and enjoy your wife's cooking, sir, but I've promised to have dinner with another gentleman today, and if I don't get back on the road soon I'll be late for my meeting with him. I don't want to be rude to him, you see."

Means looked genuinely sorry to hear that. "You plan on eating here the next time you pass this way, sir. Now I mean that, too. You plan on it."

"Mr. Means, that is a promise," Dex lied as he extended a hand for the farmer to shake. "I will make a point of it."

Dex "allowed" James to hold his stirrup as he mounted Galahad, then paused for a moment so James could clamber into the saddle of the rented roan. "Thank you, Mr. Means."

"Any time, sir. Any time at all."

Dex smiled and nodded and wheeled Galahad down the lane toward the public roadway.

· 30 ·

"You son of a bitch."

"Pardon me?"

"That buttermilk. You knew, you bastard."

"Knew what? What are you talking about? The buttermilk? I agree. It was damn good."

"I hate buttermilk. I'd rather drink cold snot than damn buttermilk."

"No!" Dex exclaimed, eyes wide and innocent. "I didn't know that."

"The hell you didn't."

"No, really. You don't like buttermilk? Damn, James, you should have said something about it."

James gave him a look that was suspicious, true, but decidedly less hostile than the first had been. "I've always hated buttermilk."

Dex spread his hands. "I'm really sorry to hear that, James. I guess I forgot."

"I still think you knew, damn you."

"No. Really." Dex gave his friend a cherubic smile and bit into a cold fried chicken wing, part of the lunch the hotel packed for them this morning. Today, he'd promised himself earlier, they were *not* going to be trapped into a day of non-stop eating no matter how hospitable and generous the would-be hosts.

The two of them were seated at the bole of a huge old oak deep in a roadside grove that was cool and refreshing after the midday heat out on the road that ran along the Neches River south of Benson.

Yesterday they had ridden north. Today they turned south. And just as James had observed yesterday, today too they passed farm after farm where one or more major pieces of equipment showed the bright, clean paint of recent purchase.

Not all the farms were so graced, of course. But an untoward number of them seemed to be.

"Debt," Dex said aloud, chewing thoughts every bit as thoroughly as he was chewing the crispy skin of his chicken wing.

"Huh?"

"The scheme Reggoner and Mullen have going for them. Debt. It has to be that."

"They want the farmers to be in debt to them?"

"That's right. I don't believe for a minute that Reggoner somehow came into possession of a bunch of cheap farm equipment. And if he ever did he isn't the sort of man who'd run around looking for strangers he could do favors for and not take any sort of profit for himself. No sir, not our boy Charles. The S.O.B. won't even pay off his gaming debts. And now we're expected to believe that he so loves his fellow man that he gives them plows and manure spreaders practically for nothing? That he even arranges interest-free loans so they can take advantage of the deals?" Dex shook his head. "I don't think so."

"You know the old saying," James said. "If it sounds too good to be true, believe it 'cause it certainly *is* too good to be true."

"Reggoner must be the one offering the equipment, and Mullen is the one with the money. That part is easy enough to see. But . . . why, dammit? Why are they going to all this trouble, James?"

"What does a man do when he's in debt?"

"Pays it off, of course. With interest."

"And if he can't pay it off?"

Dex didn't have to take much time to think that one through. "Then he's up shit creek, of course."

"Yeah, but exactly how? That's what I'm asking."

"Depends on the deal that was made, doesn't it," Dex said. "It could mean a lot of things." He stopped chewing and sat upright, no longer leaning back against the bark of the old tree. "It could mean just having to give the stuff back. The equipment the loan was made against. But . . . if a contract was signed, a mortgage like, defaulting on the loan could lead to consequences a helluva lot worse than that. Losing real property, for instance. Why, if Reggoner and Mullen wrote the notes to call for it, a man in default on an equipment loan could be required to forfeit his whole damned farm."

"That's what I was thinking, too, Dex."

"You know what I want to do?"

"Sure, I do."

"What is it that I want next?" Dex challenged.

"Hell, white boy, you're easy. You want to get a look at some of those loan agreements Reggoner and Mullen have gotten folks to sign."

"Damn, James, you aren't as dumb as you look."

"Yezzuh, bawss. Whatever you says, bawss, yezzuh."
James laughed. And reached for a plump chicken thigh.

· 31 ·

They split up for the afternoon, James offering only a rather cryptic comment about wanting to go back to one of the farms they'd visited the previous day and Dex riding back to Benson. There seemed no point in going any further south. He already knew what he would find there: more of the same. Now his question was: the same *what*? He badly wanted a look at one of the loan agreements Charles Reggoner was having his customers sign, and that very probably would require more thought rather than more travel.

He left Galahad in Henry Adams's excellent care and stopped in at the saloon where sweet Helena sometimes worked. In the absence of constructive effort a bit of mid-afternoon dalliance would not be amiss, he thought.

"I suppose it's too much to ask whether you've gotten any brandy in stock during the past day or two," Dex said, not really expecting a positive reply but mildly hopeful anyway.

"Bourbon, whiskey or rye, mister," the bartender said in a sympathetic tone of voice.

"In that case a beer. It's hot out there."

The barman nodded and reached for one of the tall tin mugs stacked ready to hand.

"I said it before," Dex heard from behind him, "and I say it again. You are no gentleman, and I owe you nothing. I advise you to stop pestering Mr. Whitcomb about things that don't concern him."

Dex accepted his beer and dropped a nickel onto the bar to pay for it. He took a swallow and set the mug carefully down again before he bothered to turn.

Charles Reggoner was still standing there. He was dressed in a dark suit and boiled shirt, but he wore neither tie nor collar on the shirt and he looked slightly flushed, as if from recent and strenuous exertion.

"That is twice you've claimed that about me, Reggoner," Dex said in a deceptively soft voice. "Your friends talked me out of receiving satisfaction the first time. They aren't here t' make you so lucky this time around."

Reggoner's lip twisted in a sneer. "You want a duel, you bastard? Fine. I'll accommodate you."

Dexter nodded solemnly. "Very well. Would tomorrow morning suffice? At dawn, say?"

"Why wait until then? You want time to scurry away with your tail tucked low, is that it? What's wrong with right now?" Reggoner's voice had risen in pitch. He spoke loudly and with emphasis, obviously wanting every man in the place to overhear his challenge and to see Yancey's responses. But then Charles Reggoner just as obviously believed it improbable that Yancey would have the nerve to actually face him.

"I see you aren't wearing a gun." Reggoner patted his own armpit. Dex assumed that indicated that he wore a gun there—which in fact Dexter did as well, although it was not a fact that he particularly wished to advertise—either that or Reggoner had body lice in his underarm hair. Dex reflected on that and concluded that it was a possibility. But more likely the man wanted to show that he was armed and ready for an encounter.

By now several gentlemen, some of them men Dex recognized from the racetrack and including Tyler Whitcomb's friend Alex Peacock, were crowding around close.

"Do you want to get a gun?" Reggoner challenged. "Or

will you crawl away on your belly like the snake you really are?"

Dex smiled and shrugged. "I don't expect I'll need a gun," he said.

Reggoner turned and gave the gentlemen of Benson a look of smug and haughty triumph. "See? I told you, I told all of you, this man is no gentleman."

"To the contrary, sir." Dex bowed slightly, first to Reggoner and then in the direction of Peacock and the others. "As the challenged party, I remind you that the choice of weapons is mine."

Reggoner looked annoyed. "What's that?"

"Very simple. You issued a challenge. I accept it, sir. Now it is my right to select the weapons to be used."

"What the hell are you talking about? Get your damn gun and reach for it whenever you want. That's what's simple."

Dexter gave the man a pained look. "Will someone please explain the proper etiquette of affairs of honor to this . . ." his hesitation was prolonged and his expression accusing, ". . . gentleman?"

"Mr. Yancey is correct, Charles. You challenged him. Now he gets to pick how you'll fight."

"We'll fight with pistols, dammit," Reggoner declared.

"Only if Mr. Yancey chooses them," Peacock corrected. "And if you do, the proper manner would have you both stand with weapons already drawn, facing at a distance to be determined by your seconds, and each firing only upon command. That, Charles, is the proper manner." Peacock turned to Dex. "What is your choice, sir?"

"I choose the epee," Dex said in a firm, clear voice.

"As you wish, sir," Peacock said.

"What the fuck is an epee?" Reggoner demanded. "Are we supposed to whip out dicks and pee on each other from ten paces?" He snorted.

"Swords, Charles. The gentleman has chosen to fight you with swords," Peacock said, his voice hinting of a bit of disgust.

"Swords? I don't know anything about fucking swords. I invited the man to fight, not to dance."

"Nevertheless, your challenge has been answered, and the gentleman has chosen the epee. It is within his right to do so."

"I'm not going to fight him with any fucking sword."

"Then you withdraw your challenge?" Peacock asked.

"Hell no. But it's pistols we'll fight with."

"Charles," another gentleman admonished, "that choice is not yours. Either you accept his choice of the sword or you must withdraw your challenge. You do not have any other options." The old gentleman's expression became resolute. "Not if you intend to remain in this community, you haven't."

Reggoner looked from one grim face to another among the men who surrounded him. Then he looked back at Dex. His face twisted with fury, but after a moment he spat, "I'm not fighting him with any fucking sword." He spun on his heels and stalked out of the saloon.

Dex watched Reggoner out of sight, then turned to the gents. "I apologize for disrupting your relaxation, gentlemen." He bowed low.

The gentlemen of Benson turned silently—embarrassed by one of their own, although Charles Reggoner did not yet seem to appreciate that fact—and returned to their card games and quiet conversations.

The talk around Benson would be affected for some days to come, Dex knew. He wondered how long it would be before Reggoner discovered the damage he'd just now done to his own reputation among the better-quality folk of the community.

◆ 32 ◆

"You look mighty damn pleased with yourself."

James's response was to grin hugely, then reach under his shirt. He pulled out a brown envelope and tossed it onto the hotel room bed at Dexter's side.

"That couldn't be . . ."

"Maybe not, but it is," James replied.

"How did you get it?"

"Remember yesterday when we stopped at the little farm upriver owned by a man named Bryant?"

Dex shook his head. "We stopped at so many places, they all run together in my mind."

"Tall man, real skinny. He raises chickens mostly and truck crops. Had a little black woman there that was doing some laundry when we came up."

"I remember him now, sure. That's where you went?"

James nodded. "There was something about him and that little woman that got my attention. For one thing, this Bryant actually looked at me when he was talking, not just at you. And the woman wasn't standing especially close beside him or anything like that, but she was listening in to everything we said. Well, everything you said. But I'd kind of got the impression that both of them would have paid attention if I'd said anything, too. Like they assumed I could have something to say, too. Both of them. That isn't normal, you know.''

Dex grunted. He certainly couldn't argue the point. After all, it was something that James had firsthand experience with while Dexter himself never could.

"I went back there this afternoon, and I was right. Mr. Bryant and Jasmine stepped over the broomstick. You know what I mean.''

"But he's white.''

"That's right. And she's black. Is there something wrong with that?''

"Dammit, James, you know that isn't what I mean. It's just that I never heard of a white man doing that. It's a slave thing.'' In the absence of lawful marriage vows for slaves, who often fell in love despite or in outright opposition to the rulings of their masters, the custom among slaves was that if a man and woman pledged themselves before others and stepped together over a broomstick they considered themselves to be married and were accepted as such by other Negroes.

"It still isn't legal for a white man to marry a black woman, you know. Not anyplace that I ever heard about, at least not in this country.''

"They're a couple then?'' Dex asked.

"He really loves her, Dex. It isn't one of those things where the white man is lording it over some poor little ol' black gal. These two people really love each other.''

"I didn't notice,'' Dex admitted.

"They don't want anyone to know. The folks around here think he's just an old bachelor with no interest in women and think Jasmine is his housekeeper. The Bryants want everyone to keep on thinking that way so they'll be left alone. They worked it all out right in the very beginning. They put on their kind of act in public just like you and I do.'' James grinned. "Except we don't have to worry about one of us getting the other pregnant.''

"If you try and touch me, you black son of a bitch . . .''

James laughed. "The Bryants decided early on they

daren't have children. It wouldn't be fair to the kids if they did. But Dex, I'll tell you something. I don't think I've ever met two people who appreciate each other more than Jasmine and Ed Bryant do.''

"For two people who want to hide their relationship from the world they sure opened right up to you," Dex observed.

"It's my boyish charm," James said modestly.

"Plus what else?"

"I kind of let them know that I'd already guessed. And then I came clean with them about you and I being friends. I wanted them to know that we have to share some of the same things that they do. I hope you don't mind me doing that, Dex.''

"You know I trust your judgment. Go on."

"We sat in their kitchen and had a nice visit. And I'll tell you something else, Dex. Ed Bryant treated me like a guest in his house. A white man, and he treated me like a real guest. It was . . . it's different with you. You know? We've been together as long as either one of us can remember. But Bryant . . . it wasn't important to him that I'm black. He had me sit down at his table like company. Hell, not like 'as if.' To him I really *was* company. He wasn't putting on any act for Jasmine's benefit. He was just . . . nice. You know?''

Dex nodded. If he did not completely know what James felt about that at least he could imagine it. He could come close to knowing.

"We had a nice visit, like I said, and I went ahead and told the Bryants what we were interested in. Ed didn't hesitate a bit. He looked at Jasmine and raised his eyebrows and she looked back at him and nodded her head. They each of them knew what the other was thinking. They didn't have to say it out loud. And then Jasmine got up and went inside their bedroom for a minute, and when she came out again she had this envelope. She handed it over to me and sat down close beside her husband. I told them we would look it over and I'd get the document back to them as soon as I could.''

"I'll make a copy this evening," Dex said. "I don't suppose they'd mind that. No names, though. I'll leave those out just in case we ever want to show the copy to anyone. Then you can take the original back to the Bryants tomorrow first thing."

"They're nice folks, Dex. I'd sure as hell hate to see any harm come to them."

"I won't do anything that would . . ."

"It isn't us I'm thinking about, Dex. It's Reggoner and his friend George Mullen. If they're scheming something hurtful to the families that've signed these equipment loans . . . dammit, Dex, I want to stop them from it. Over and above what happened to Saladin even, I want to stop them."

"Then let's see first can we figure out what they're up to, James. After that we'll see can we do something about it."

Dex reached for the envelope and slid the flap open.

• 33 •

"You know what's been bothering me?" James asked.

Dex grinned at him. "Of course I do. Same thing that was bothering me to start with."

James gave him a skeptical look.

"The date. Why so far off. Why hold back all the way until next spring. Am I right?"

"You're right," James admitted. He sounded disappointed.

Dex's grin grew wider. "I think I have the deal figured out now. Might have a few picky little details wrong, but I think I know what they're up to. And why they didn't write these agreements so they could call the notes in early."

"Then you're ahead of me on this one, Dexter," James said.

"See? Whites really are superior."

James picked up a pillow and took aim but at the last moment decided against flinging it. He settled for, "Later. I'll get you later, ofay."

"Sure you will," Dex said cheerfully. Although he knew that James probably would get back at him later. Somehow and some way. James had a fine memory, especially when it came to something like this. But that was not the point at the moment.

"What I think is that Reggoner—or more likely Mullen since I think he's the brainy one of the pair—figured that the farmers would be wary of any note that could be called in early. Even without interest and at an unbelievably low price they'd be suspicious if Reggoner tried to put anything like that in the language. They would think he was gulling them—which of course he is—and back away rather than sign a deal that could catch them with their pockets empty. So Mullen and Reggoner wrote their contracts with a date-certain for repayment of the loan. To allay suspicion."

"Oh, I got that much myself," James said. "But why give the farmers so *much* time to come up with the payment. Why would they wait until next spring? If it's really the land that your white friends want, why wait all that long to get their hands on it?"

"A couple reasons," Dex said. "We both agree that it's the land that they want, right?"

James nodded. "Sure. It's all bottom land that they seem to be interested in. We're only seeing Reggoner's bright new equipment on the farms along the Neches. At all of the places we've visited back away from the river, all the spreaders and plows and stuff have been your usual collection of beat-up junk. No tell-tale bright paint on any of them."

"Right. But bottom land around here is worth, what— four dollars an acre? five?"

"Bottom land goes high everywhere," James said. "I can ask Ed and Jasmine what it's worth here these days, but I'd say you're probably guessing in the right neighborhood at four or five dollars an acre."

"Exactly. And this," Dex tapped the brown envelope that held the Bryants' loan agreement, "this loan would work out to maybe a dollar an acre or less if you calculated it out."

"About that, sure."

"So the boys figure they can run this scheme and get

their hands on prime bottom land for a dollar an acre, then turn around and sell it for four or five times what they invested. If I can use that word for their larceny even though it shouldn't rightly apply. What they're doing is cheating people out of their life's work just for the sake of a few dollars in profit.

"And hell, even if some of the farmers do pay off the loans, Reggoner and Mullen won't be hurt. They won't collect interest, but I'll bet what they've done is get a wholesale rate on the equipment they're providing. Buy cheap and sell it on at cost just to toll in the suckers, right?"

James nodded. "That sounds reasonable."

"And at that rate, let's say some of the intended victims actually pay off the loan. Mullen and company don't win. But they don't lose anything either. It's like being dealt a push at the blackjack table. No gain, no loss, no harm done and you're ready to deal again."

"You still haven't said anything about why they're waiting all the way until spring to have these notes come due," James objected.

"Think about it for a minute."

"I have been, dammit."

"So think about it some more. They benefit two ways by waiting that long. No, now that I think about it they benefit three different ways. First, it helps entice the suckers to begin with because the terms are so generous. No early call on the note and they have all the way into next year to repay. Plenty of time. No pressure. A man is going to like that. It will make him feel good about being able to come up with the money."

"All right, I can accept that. We'll call it your first reason. One down and two to go."

"Two," Dex said. "Fall harvest time is the normal period when a farmer has some money in his pockets, and most farm loans come due in the fall just after harvest when a man is best able to repay. Right?"

"Exactly," James agreed.

"By waiting until spring for their notes to come due, Reggoner and Mullen anticipate that a good many of those

farmers won't have enough self-control to put the loan repayment into a cigar box under the hearth or wherever else
and leave that money the hell alone. The boys are counting
on ordinary human nature, James. If a man has money in
his pocket, he is damn sure gonna spend it. Especially a
man who usually *doesn't* have money to spare.

"He'll want to buy his wife a new dress. Just one. What
could that hurt? Probably she hasn't had a nice new hat
and dress in years. So he'll buy her one. And maybe a new
pipe for himself and a couple pairs of britches and shoes
for the kids. And the next thing you know, half that money
is gone and there isn't enough left to pay the note off.

"So the guy tells himself that that nice Mr. Reggoner
will surely accept half in the spring and let him carry over
just a lousy few more months until fall again for the rest
of his money. He can offer to pay interest on the extension,
and Mr. Reggoner is such a swell fellow that he's sure to
go along with that plan. Except of course Mr. Reggoner
will do no such thing. He'll cackle and grin and foreclose
on the poor S.O.B.'s note like a scratch hen snapping up a
junebug. Peck, peck, now I got your land, sucker."

James pondered that explanation for a moment, then nodded. "I can buy that, sure. Like you say, it's human nature.
They won't get everyone to spend away their repayment
money, but they'll probably get enough to make the game
worthwhile." He stretched, stood up and began getting
dressed. "That's two. So what is your third reason?"

Dex grinned. "Greed, of course. The boys . . . and I'll
thank you to not call them mine; I don't claim the sons of
bitches . . . the boys want every last penny they can squeeze
out of those poor bastards."

"Which means?" James tucked his shirttail into his trousers and pulled the galluses over his shoulders, then sat
back down on the side of the bed and began putting his
shoes on.

"When do property taxes usually come due?" Dex asked
by way of an answer.

"I'll be damned," James said. "I think you're right.
They want to take over those farms right after the taxes

have been paid. Save themselves the bother. And the money.''

"Exactly. And I think there's even a fourth reason, sort of," Dex added. "It's easier to sell a farm if you show it when there's a crop already in the field and it all looks green and fine from someone else's work. Buyers would pay top dollar and be happy to get the deal. Most foreclosed farms come available because the previous owner went bust from being a lousy farmer. Worse, the last years that a man like that holds his farm he's cutting every corner he can, trying to save money. His fences and equipment and everything are in poor repair, and the place looks generally like hell. These farms are being run by men who are for the most part good and careful husbandmen. They'll be a damn sight nicer than run of the mill foreclosures. Easy to sell and priced at the top end of the range.''

"Those bastards," James said.

"What, that's a big surprise to you?"

"No, but it's . . . cold-blooded. It's just plain cruel.''

"Stealing generally is," Dex responded.

"You think there's anything we can do about it?" James asked.

"My friend, I damn well guarantee you we can put a curb on them. I don't have a doubt in the world about that. My only problem is trying to figure out how we can come out of it with some of Reggoner's and Mullen's money in *our* pockets.''

"You have something in mind about this?"

Dex's grin was positively huge. "Sit back down and listen. I think you're gonna like this."

· 34 ·

"I like them," Dex said, walking around the horses that James was holding. "I like them a lot, Mr. Adams."

"I told you I'd do right by you," the livery man said with a note of pride. "An' I'll tell you something else. If you're going to be around for a few more days, make it a point to use them. Ride them out. If you think they're unsound for any reason, or for no reason at all, you bring them back, one or the both of them, and I'll keep on looking until I find something you do like."

"I trust they are both as sound as you obviously believe them to be," Dex said. "I don't expect they will come back except to stand in your barn."

"In that case maybe you'd like to have your boy there saddle them while you join me inside. I have the papers all prepared for you to sign, transferring your horse to Mr. Whitcomb, and of course I have bills of sale for you on both of these."

The animals the liveryman proposed to exchange for poor, slow Galahad were each and either a far cry better horse than he was. Intended for Dex's own use was a leggy black gelding with good bones, a deep chest and a shallow angle of the shoulder, which indicated it would be smooth and easy at the trot. If there was as much as one white hair to be found anywhere on the animal, Dex hadn't yet spotted it.

The second horse, intended for James's use, was dark, bloodred in the forequarters but with a blanket of white on his rump. The expanse of white was dotted with spots, both black and the same dark shade of red that covered most of the horse. The animal also had rings of pale, near-white hair around its eyes, and the eyes were a somewhat disconcerting blue.

The bill of sale on the rather strange-looking spotted horse showed that it had somehow come to Texas all the way from the Oregon country.

Dex was skeptical about the animal. It damn sure looked funny. But Adams assured him it was sound and could see just fine. "It's a tough little son of a bitch," Adams promised. "Not fast and not smart . . . not that any horse really is . . . but you can't hardly wear the little bastard out or even make it break a sweat. Tell you the truth, I likely would have recommended it for your horse except it wouldn't be seemly for a white man to have to sit and look up to a nigger."

"Of course," Dex said. "Thank you." He did not think it appropriate to mention to the livery man that Saladin had stood a good three fingers taller than Galahad and neither he nor James had cared a fig.

Between these two, Dex's black was about two fingers the taller.

"The man I got the Oregon horse from said they're called Poosa horses or something like that. The white blanket and spots are supposed to be there, and the eyes most all look like that, too. Or anyhow that's what the man said. I never heard of such a horse, but he seemed honest enough."

"It's the soundness that I care about," Dex told him, "not what they look like."

Adams nodded sagely. "You know what the prettiest color is for a horse," he said and without waiting for a response provided the time-honored answer. "It's fat. If

you got good health underneath the hide, the color and
markings don't matter a lick.''

Dex nodded. This was hardly the first time he'd heard
that truism, but repetition could not discredit what was so
to begin with.

Adams presented him with a short but correct bill of sale
for Galahad and delivered to Dex the ownership papers
describing the two new horses, each duly signed by the
previous owners and attested to by a Notary Public.

"Do you want me to go with you to the Notary for this
signature too?" Dex asked as he rather happily signed Galahad away.

"No need, son. My nephew over at the courthouse is a
Notary. He'll take care of it for me if you've no objection.''

"What does your nephew do there?''

"Works in the County Clerk's office,'' Adams told him.

Dex tucked the information away for future reference.
Just in case he and James found themselves in need either
of a Notary or of a source of information inside the courthouse.

He stood and shook Henry Adams's hand. "You've been
a big help, sir, and I thank you.''

"My pleasure,'' Adams said. "Will you be staying on
for a while then?''

"Quite possibly until the end of the year,'' Dex said.

"Oh really? I sort of had the idea you were just passing
through.''

Dex smiled at him. "Not until my business here is
done,'' he said.

"Mind if I ask what that business is, Mr. Yancey?''

Dex laughed. "I don't mind the question if you don't
mind my reluctance to answer it.'' He laid a finger beside
his nose and winked, and Adams chuckled, too.

"Like that is it, young man? Well rest assured. I'll not
say a word to anyone. Not a word, sir.''

Dex rather heartily hoped that Adams would at the very
least say something about his secretiveness. And about the
proposed length of his stay in Benson.

Which, come to think of it, he told himself, he must

remember soon to make clear to the people at the hotel as well. Perhaps he should discuss with them a reduced room rate based on length of stay. That would help get the word out so that Charles Reggoner and George Mullen might learn of it.

"Thank you, sir. Thank you very much," Dex said again, then went outside to mount his tall horse and get on with the day. James, he thought, would just have to suffer along on the shorter, stouter animal.

· 35 ·

Dex remembered the place when he saw it. James led the way, guiding his funny-looking spotted horse down a shaded lane to a small collection of farm buildings. The Bryant house was small but tidy with bright red flowers—geraniums? Dex scarcely knew one blossom from another—in window boxes on either side of the front door, and the barn and other buildings were clean and in good repair.

Chickens by the score darted underfoot, squawking and flapping their useless wings and raising a hell of a row. It would be difficult for strangers to come near unnoticed, at least during daylight. Dex could see some guinea fowl scratching for bugs in the garden plot, so the place was probably protected by those shrill sentinels at night, too.

A small, dark face appeared at the barn doorway in response to all the commotion. Dex did not remember the woman, but it had to be Jasmine Bryant. She smiled broadly and called out when she saw who the visitors were.

"Hello, James. We didn't expect to see you again so soon. Step down and come inside. Bring your friend with you."

Now that was a first, James being welcomed instead of Dexter. They tied the horses to an empty hay rick and entered the cool, shadowy interior of the Bryants' small barn.

The barn was divided into pens along the right-hand wall and three stalls on the left. A pair of mules and a very large horse stood in the stalls while the pens contained grossly fat sows, each with a litter of small pigs. Ed Bryant and his wife had been interrupted in the midst of doing something with the pigs and with muttered apologies returned to their task now.

Dex felt a momentary flutter of discomfort low in his belly when he saw what the day's work was. Bryant's hands were bloody and he held a small pen knife. Jasmine, presumably the quicker of the two of them, was catching the piglets, dropping the young gelts into a separate pen immediately but holding the boar pigs dangling by their hind legs and offering them to her husband.

With two quick practice strokes of his little knife, Ed Bryant sliced open the pig's sack and squeezed its testes out so he could reach them. He pulled them free and dropped them into a container.

"Good timing," Ed Bryant said while he waited for his wife to deposit that little boar-turned-barrow in with the females and other newly castrated males and grab the next victim. "You would be Dexter."

"Yes, sir. Nice to see you again," Dex said. He did remember the man now. Sort of.

"James told us about you." The tall farmer smiled. "I'd offer to shake hands, Mr. Yancey, but I'm covered with blood. Don't want to get you all sticky with it."

Dex knew how to be polite when he wanted to. He stuck his hand out in spite of the warning and shook with the farmer. He could wash the gore off later. "It's good of you to be so trusting with us," he said. "Thank you for letting James borrow that loan agreement."

"We have no secrets, Mr. Yancey," Bryant said with a grin and a sideways glance toward his wife. Her skin color was even darker than James's, and she was not especially pretty. Ed Bryant quite obviously cared about neither of those things. She was his woman, and that was that. "Well, none worth speaking of," he concluded with a wink.

"Or anyway none worth repeating," Dex said by way of pledging his own silence on the matter.

"We brought your contract back," James said. "We did copy it off in Dex's hand. I hope that's all right with you."

"I left out your name," Dex put in.

"It's quite all right by us, with my name on it or not. Jasmine and I aren't much frightened by anything that is true. There are things more important than the few dollars involved in that loan."

Jasmine came back with a frantically squealing pig in hand—poor little son of a bitch really would've squealed, Dex thought, if he'd known what was about to happen—and Bryant excused himself for a moment while he turned another male pig into an "it" that would grow faster and be less aggressive with its penmates than a whole male would.

Dex winced when he saw Bryant's knife slice into the tiny, puckered pouch that contained the little fellow's balls. There were times, he reflected, when it was damned uncomfortable to have an active imagination.

"Unfortunately, sir," Dex said when he had Bryant's attention again, "we don't think the word 'few' would be appropriate when you talk about the dollars that are involved in this thing."

"No? We borrow less than two hundred dollars in that note, as you already saw for yourself. And the truth is, Jasmine is very careful with our money. I don't mind telling you that we can afford to repay the note from savings no matter what else might arise. I only agreed to accept the note to begin with because that was one of Mr. Reggoner's conditions for selling us the equipment at cost. He said something about having to be able to show the transfers on paper. Although he never did say to whom he needed to show the sales or why."

"We think we know why," James said.

Jasmine returned with another piglet, and Dex shuddered all over again even though this time he turned his face away and didn't look. He heard the tiny, moist sound of the testes dropping into the pot with all the rest and resolved that no matter how hospitable these people were, he was *not* going to stay for dinner here. He had all too good an idea of what they would be serving for lunch, and he wanted none of it, thank you.

While James explained what he and Dex had deduced about Reggoner and his plan, Dex went outside for a breath of clean air. He'd been feeling just a wee bit woozy inside the barn for a moment there. Not enough air circulation, he supposed, and never mind that the big double doors stood open at the front while another was open to a small feedlot behind the building.

"If you're right about this," Jasmine was saying when Dex returned, "it's a good thing we can't get caught up in debt and lose our place."

"I'm sure Reggoner and his partner Mullen know they won't succeed with everyone who accepted their notes," James said. "We've talked about that. But we are just as sure—and believe that Reggoner and Mullen are counting on it too—that not all of your neighbors will have been so careful."

Dex repeated his example of the housewife's new dress and hat and just a few little extras for the kids. "I'll wager that a good percentage of the folks who have their payment ready in the fall won't still have that in the bank come the spring," he said.

"Unfortunately, you are very probably right about that," Bryant said.

"We should do something to warn them," Jasmine immediately added.

"I'm not so sure," Bryant said. "People around here already think I'm something of a strange duck. I don't know that they would appreciate me poking my nose into their private affairs like this."

"We can't sit by and allow our neighbors to be harmed, Edwin," Jasmine said firmly. "We would be responsible for their sorrow if we knew what lay ahead and did nothing to help."

Bryant opened his mouth to speak, but his wife wagged a finger under his nose to hush him before he could get the

words out. "No excuses, Edwin Bryant. I know what you
want to say, and I'll not hear it out of your mouth. Everyone who wants an easy way out of a difficult situation with
his neighbors falls back on the old question 'Am I my
brother's keeper?' Somehow they always forget that the
answer to that question is, 'Yes, I am.' So I'll listen to no
excuses, mister. We will have to come up with some way
to warn our neighbors."

Dex smiled. "Now I'm real pleased to hear you say that,
Mrs. Bryant, because that right there was one of the things
we wanted to talk with you about this morning."

"You have something in mind, sir?" Bryant asked.

James grinned. "Since you mention it, Ed, yes sir, in
fact we do. D'you want to tell him, Dex, or shall I?"

Dex was feeling woozy again. He'd been staring at the
pen knife in Ed Bryant's bloody hand and was feeling just
the least bit dizzy. "You tell him," Dex blurted as he scur-
ried for the fresh air outdoors. He got out of sight just
barely in time to fertilize some of Jasmine's flowers with
the barely used remains of what had been a rather enjoyable
hotel breakfast.

Inside the barn he could hear the drone of conversation,
but right at that particular moment he didn't much care
what was being said or by whom.

⋅ 36 ⋅

"Come on, Dex, it's not that late," James prodded.

"The point isn't the hour, dammit, it's that I'm tired. I'm not some low-life field hand like some people I know. I'm not used to having to do," he shivered and made a face, "work."

"Lazy white bastard."

"Yes, I am. So what's your point?" Dex demanded.

James laughed and began to pack away their "instrument."

The instrument was something Ed and Jasmine had enthusiastically—and rather gleefully—come up with once they understood the direction Dex and James wanted to take with their half-formed plan.

None of the four of them knew the first thing about surveying. But then it was unlikely that anyone else up and down this stretch of the Neches River would really understand it either.

Jasmine had come up with an impressively large brass tube with an eyepiece at one end and a frosted glass at the large end. The item was in fact a long-ago broken kaleidoscope that no longer held the mirrors and bits of colored glass that once made it work. But the brass device still looked imposing and official and in all rather grand.

Ed fabricated a tripod to mount the old kaleidoscope upon, and even found a plumb bob to suspend beneath the head of the phony instrument. "I don't know why they have them, but I saw some surveyors at work once, and they had plumb bobs attached to the gadgets they were using. Shooting lines is what I think they called whatever it was they were doing."

"Shooting lines? I wonder what that means."

Bryant shrugged.

James grinned and suggested, "If anybody asks what it means, you'll just have to give them a pitying look like as if to say that any fool ought to know that much."

"Isn't there supposed to be something out in the distance for these guys to look *at*?" Dex asked.

"Darned if I'd know," Bryant admitted.

"Don't ask me," James said. "I'm just a po' darky bein' led astray."

"You should hear this poor little old colored boy go into his act. Has a mouth that's plumb full of mush, he does."

"Don't worry about what you're supposed to be looking at," Jasmine said, getting back to business. "Not that you can see through this old thing anyway. But nobody else will know that. And you want to mystify them anyway, so if anyone asks you questions just act snotty. Can he handle that, James?"

"Why, my friend Dexter there has been practicing acting snotty his whole life long."

"I object to that," Dex said.

"On what grounds?"

"Because I haven't yet lived my whole life. So how can you claim I'm acting snotty the whole time?"

"He has a point," Bryant agreed.

"I knew you'd side with the white man," Jasmine said with a jab to her husband's ribs. "When push comes to shove . . ."

"Don't be uppity," Bryant chided. And quickly ducked to avoid a playfully thrown clod. At least Dex assumed that

Jasmine was being playful. She must have been, though, to have missed so widely.

In the long run, Dexter and James rode away from the Bryant farm armed with a large and businesslike device that anyone who did not know better should surely mistake for a precision surveying instrument.

They'd spent the remainder of the day going from farm to farm along the river, stopping to ask permission to trespass in the fields and all the river banks, then moving from place to place—always within plain sight of anyone who happened near—setting up the tripod and peering studiously into the brass barrel of the defunct kaleidoscope. Every once in a while Dex would expand upon their charade by pausing to take out a notepad and jot down entirely meaningless figures in it.

The best part of the day though, at least as far as Dex was concerned, was that Jasmine had been understanding and generous and kind. She'd accepted his all-too-transparent excuses and not pressed them to stay for lunch, even though James had made clear that he for one thoroughly enjoyed the delicate flavor of fried pig nuts.

Cheese sandwiches provided by the hotel were much more palatable as far as Dex was concerned. And they stayed down, too.

Now, late in the afternoon, they packed up their gaudy instrument and turned the horses back toward Benson.

· 37 ·

Dex kissed the nape of Helena's pretty neck. He felt the girl quiver at the touch of his tongue. She was face down on the bed with Dex stretched out half on top of her. He moved over a bit so that his body covered hers. Her butt—cute it was and very nicely rounded—pressed against his erection. He could feel his shaft nested warm and pleasantly between the cheeks of her ass.

"Spread your legs a little wider, please." He nuzzled the back of her neck again.

"I . . . I'll do it if'n you really want, Dex honey, but let me get some sweet butter t'rub on first so's it don't hurt quite so bad. Please?"

Dex kissed her again. "Thank you, dear, but that isn't what I had in mind."

"You ain't gonna cornhole me?"

"No, I ain't. I just want to enter from back here. Okay?"

She sighed, obviously happy with his explanation, and quickly moved her legs apart and lifted her hips to accommodate his entry. Dex slid inside her easily, enjoying the sensations of her moist heat engulfing and encompassing his own very sensitive flesh.

"That feels good, honey," Helena whispered, wriggling her hips and giggling just a little.

"Mm, I agree. Close your legs tight together now. Yes, like that. Ah, that's nice. Nicer than nice."

"You like this angle?"

"Yes."

"How 'bout this one?"

"It's good."

"But the other's better?"

"Yes," he admitted. "A little."

"There. Like that?"

"Exactly like that."

He licked the back of her neck and felt the girl's reaction, leaned down lower and played the tip of his tongue inside her ear.

"God, I like that," Helena said.

"Good, because so do I."

"Dexter honey, could I ask you something?"

"Of course."

"Would you . . . I know this is an awful thing to ask of a fella, and I want you should know I wouldn't ask it of anybody else I've ever met, not in my whole life, I wouldn't."

"I'm flattered by your confidence in me, dear. Now what is your request?"

"I been timing my periods. My monthlies. You know?"

He nodded. She was not in a position to see the gesture, but he knew she would be able to feel the movement against her hair. He kissed her neck again very lightly.

"The way I figure it, Dexter, I oughta be fertile along about the middle of next week."

"Yes?"

"Dexter honey, I wouldn't hold you liable for nothing. Wouldn't make no claims on you. I promise you that. Besides, you'll be moving on. This ain't your kind of place, and you won't stay. I know that, an' what I'm asking isn't for permanent like. It's just . . ."

"Yes?"

"Dexter honey, would you come by here Wednesday night an' fuck me?"

"Pardon?"

"I want a baby, Dexter. I want a little baby t' love an' care for. I got no family in the world no more, an' I know I'll never ever be able to marry. I'm not complaining, mind. I knew what I was about when I decided t' get into this business. But I'm pretty good at what I do."

"You are that, sweetheart," he assured her.

"An' I can earn enough t' keep myself an' a baby, too. I'd raise it fine, Dexter. Teach it right from wrong an' see that it goes t' church every Sunday. I'd make a good mama, Dexter. I promise you that. I'd take care of it real good. An' I'd like for you to be the daddy. So . . . will you come around and do me again on Wednesday? Free, of course. You'd be doin' me a favor. I wouldn't charge you nothing and I'll do you twenty times if you're up to it. But I'll be fertile that night, I think, an' the only thing I ask is that you come in my pussy that night. I mean, I'll lick you and suck you in my ass even if that's what you want. But whenever you come that night, would you please come in my pussy and not noplace else? Please?"

"Dear girl, you do indeed flatter me."

"Will you do it then?"

"I would be honored."

Helena squealed—not so loudly as Bryant's pigs had done and much happier sounding—and wriggled her butt, the effect of which was entirely delightful as he was still socketed deep inside her body. "You'll do it? Honest?"

"Honest," he said and with a smile added, "and if I may make a suggestion, dear, I think we should practice beforehand."

"Like along about now?"

"It sounds like a fine idea to me," he agreed.

Helena laughed. She sounded very pleased, and said, "Tell you what, honey. You hold yourself over me just a bit. There, that's nice. Now hold still. Don't you move. Not a wiggle, you hear. You stay just like you are an' let me do the humping for the both of us. Hold yourself back an' try not to come just as long as you can. I'll bring you off. I promise. But if you try not to, it'll feel powerful good for you when you do squirt, you hear?''

''I hear,'' he said.

And in truth the girl was right. So much so that ''powerful'' seemed hardly adequate to describe the exquisite sensation that very quickly overwhelmed him and sent his seed spurting into her.

Ah, he thought minutes after as he lay spent and trembling on the girl's small body, the sacrifices a man has to make when he's hard at work.

✦ 38 ✦

Dex lay with two down pillows plumped behind his neck, half a water glass of excellent brandy—he had *no* idea where she'd found it—in his left hand and Helena's tit nestled warm and soft in the palm of his right hand as his arm lay draped around the girl's shoulders.

He was contented.

Also depleted. It would take him a while to recuperate. Which was perfectly all right by him. They had all night.

"Helena, dear."

"Yes, Dexter?" She nuzzled the side of his neck.

"Could we discuss business for a minute?"

"Sure, honey. Anything you want."

"I need a favor, Helena."

"You know I'd do 'most anything for you, honey. An' you don't have t' pay me if you're short or even if you just don't feel like it. You know? You're special to me, Dexter."

He smiled and kissed her, knowing good and well that she especially liked kissing. It was, after all, what made the girl feel so strongly about him, and in truth he was counting on that to help convince her she should agree to the little service he needed from her.

"Oh, you will be well rewarded if you do this for me, dear. Twice over, I should think."

"I don't know what you mean, Dexter honey."

"That's all right, little dear. Just hear me out before you make any promises. Now then . . . the first thing. Do you happen to know a man in Benson named George Mullen?"

Dex's voice droned softly on into the night.

· 39 ·

The first indication that his and James's efforts were bearing fruit came on Friday afternoon when a gap-toothed youngster in knee britches and a cloth cap came hurrying to Dex's side immediately upon Dex returning to the hotel.

Dex was tired. He'd spent a long, hard day riding up and down the Neches, dismounting every now and then to press his eye to a broken kaleidoscope and make incomprehensible hand gestures.

"You're Mr. Yancey, aren't you, sir?"

"I am, son."

"I have a message for you, sir." The boy dug deep into a pocket and extracted a crumpled and slightly sweat-dampened small envelope. "I'm to wait for your answer if you don't mind, sir."

Dex nodded and carefully ripped the end off the envelope, blew into it and with two fingers extracted a folded slip of paper.

B. TYLER WHITCOMB REQUESTS THE HONOR OF YOUR PRESENCE AT DINNER ON SATURDAY, 16TH INST., 8 O'CLOCK POST MERIDIAN. HUMBLY,

and signed with a scrawl of initials.

Tyler's house. Dex hadn't expected the overtures to come from that angle, but it did make sense now that he thought about it. Tyler was George Mullen's business partner and presumably his friend as well. He would surely agree to a dinner party if his friend and partner were to suggest one, especially if the avowed purpose were to mend fences or something along that line. Dex believed Whitcomb's involvement would be straightforward and innocent. As for Mullen, however, that would be a different matter entirely.

Dex folded the note and returned it to the envelope, which he then tucked away in his own pocket. He pulled out a handful of coins, selected a dime from among them and gave it to the boy. "Please tell Mr. Whitcomb that Mr. Yancey would be honored to attend."

The boy looked blankly toward the ceiling for a moment. His lips moved as he silently repeated the words to himself. Then he grinned and nodded. "Yes, sir. I'll tell him. Thank you, sir." He bobbed his head and spun to race away onto the street and across it to the bank building.

"Is everything satisfactory, Mr. Yancey?" the hotel clerk asked.

"Very much so, John. Thank you."

"Your laundry came back this afternoon, Mr. Yancey. Will you send your nigger down for it or would you like me to have a boy carry it up now?"

"Send it up now, please."

"Very good, sir."

Funny, Dex thought, how it always bothered him more to hear James referred to in such a disrespectful manner than it seemed to bother James himself.

But then James was used to it. It was something he had to deal with every day of his life and always would.

Besides, appearances can be deceiving.

Dex knew that quite as well as any man.

In fact, he was counting on it.

He went upstairs to wait for James to return from the livery, where he'd been left to tend to the horses. He wanted to talk with James about what they should expect come tomorrow night at Whitcomb's dinner and how Dex should react to each of the possibilities they might envision beforehand.

◆ 40 ◆

"Hold still, dammit."

"Yes, mother," Dex said.

James fiddled with the knot of Dex's bow tie again, twisting it this way and tugging it that.

"It's too tight."

"Balls. It's perfect. Now remember not to move your head."

"The whole evening?"

"That's right. Still as a cigar store Indian, that's you."

"Hard to eat that way."

"It's the price you have to pay to be a dandy white boy. Good thing is, us low-lifes don't have to put up with this shit."

"Yeah, well if we don't think of some way to keep coming up with money, I may join you in being a low-life."

"We'll think of something. It will all come out fine."

"Where'd you hear a stupid idea like that?" Dex asked, remembering quite good and well that it was his own reassurance that James was quoting back to him now.

James tilted his head one way and then the other, peering closely at Dex. Dexter's coat and trousers were freshly brushed. He wore a clean shirt and brand-new collar. He

owned two vests and was wearing the fancier of them now.
He was turned out for the evening in the best outfit he could
carry in luggage severely limited by the needs of constant
travel, although if he'd been back home on the plantation
in Louisiana . . . but that was impossible to him now and
best not thought about.

"You'll do," James said.

"Your enthusiasm overwhelms me."

"Just do what we decided on."

"I remember. Keep my mouth shut and my ears open."

"And smile a lot," James added.

"Easy, that's me."

"I know," James said, "and it worries me." He grinned.

"Wish me luck tonight."

"Luck, hell. Just remember everything so you can tell
me all about it afterward."

"D'you want me to take notes?"

"Sure, but don't be obvious about it."

Dex took a moment to admire himself in the mirror.
Thought about readjusting the tie one last time but recon-
sidered; to move it again would draw a howl from James.
Finally, he tugged at the sleeves of his coat and accepted
the dove gray planter's hat from James and placed it at a
jaunty angle.

"So let's see what happens, eh?" Dex marched downstairs and out to the waiting carriage that Tyler Whitcomb
had sent to collect him.

· 41 ·

Dex relinquished his hat and cane to a maid in a black dress and white apron, then allowed himself to be shepherded into the parlor for introductions.

He had been to Whitcomb's home before, on the morning Saladin was found dead and Sheriff Mickens did not want to do anything about it, but Dex hadn't come inside then, nor had he paid any particular attention to the place.

By Louisiana standards, Tyler Whitcomb's house would be considered decent enough, but certainly not grand. By the standards of Benson, Texas, it was grand indeed. Three stories with covered verandahs all the way around on the ground floor. A carriage house with living quarters for the servants above. A dining room glittering with chandeliers and crystal teardrops. And a parlor filled with guests for this particular occasion.

The first ones Dex noticed were the Mullens, both George and Amanda, and the lovely redhead's brother, Charles Reggoner.

Why was it he was not surprised to see them there?

Tyler greeted him with great warmth and a hearty handshake, then led Dex around the periphery of the room, performing introductions. He managed quite gracefully to save the Mullens and Reggoner for last.

"I know you've already met George and Charles. The lady is George's bride, Amanda Mullen."

Dex bowed to Amanda but refrained from extending his hand to either of the men. He did not want to seem overly eager about this nor suspiciously quick to forgive.

He found it especially interesting that Reggoner was present. Last night he and James had discussed that possibility and gave it only a three to one shot against Mullen having his brother-in-law on hand for this first overture of peace. But here the S.O.B. was. Dex gave him a glare of blatant disapproval.

Reggoner leaped immediately into his act, very probably having been coached just as thoroughly by Mullen last night as Dex was by James.

"Mr. Yancey, I want to apologize to you. I have no excuses save that I have been under much pressure lately. I haven't been myself. That does not at all justify my behavior, but I do want you to know that I regret my intemperate and ungentlemanly acts. I beg your forgiveness, sir. Also . . . and I know this is of much less importance to you than the slights to your honor have been . . . I want you to know that I have already placed on deposit at the bank a full measure of my financial obligation to you. I was very much in the wrong about that, sir. I proposed the wager, and I lost. I acknowledge that."

"And your view of whether I am or am not a gentleman, sir?" Dex pressed sternly.

Reggoner bowed. "Without question, Mr. Yancey, you are a gentleman of breeding and integrity."

"I accept your apology, Mr. Reggoner." Dex extended his hand now. He did not, however, venture any opinion as to Charles Reggoner's breeding or the man's integrity. Obligation, after all, extends only so far.

Tyler Whitcomb was beaming. So, for that matter, was George Mullen.

"Excellent," Whitcomb exclaimed. "This promises to

be a most wonderful evening, gentlemen. Simply marvelous.''

Later, when dinner was announced, Dex found himself seated on the right hand of the delectable Amanda Reggoner Mullen. He found himself wondering whose idea that had been.

But on the other hand, he really did not care. He was grateful for the favor, however it was obtained.

· 42 ·

First thing Monday morning Dex presented himself at the bank.

"I'm sorry, Mr. Yancey. Mr. Whitcomb hasn't arrived yet."

"Oh, I'm sure you can take care of my request. I believe there was a deposit made in my name recently?"

The teller smiled and nodded. "Indeed there was, sir. Would you like to take that now?"

"Please. In currency, if you will. In hundreds."

"Of course, sir. If you would step over here please and sign the receipt, I'll have it for you in a moment."

So far, Dex thought, so good.

He was especially pleased when he considered how Charles Reggoner must have groaned and grumbled about having to part with the money.

Monday afternoon Dex, James and the much-traveled kaleidoscope made their way down the lane to Ed and Jasmine Bryant's farm. They were greeted with enthusiasm.

"I managed to talk with most of the people involved," Ed Bryant told them. "I do wish you'd let me explain everything to them fully, though. I feel as if I'm deceiving them this way.''

"Ed, you *are* deceiving them. There's no help for that. We know we can trust you and Jasmine to keep a secret. Lord knows you have enough practice at it. But what about all these others? We can't take the chance. One slip of the tongue, one word to the wrong person, and the whole thing falls flat on its face. We can't risk it.''

"We've talked about that every mealtime since you were last here,'' Jasmine put in. "We understand the necessity. It is just that . . .''

"You regret it,'' Dex provided.

"Yes. We do.''

"I'm sure you regret the need to keep your relationship secret also. But you do it.''

Jasmine sighed. "And we will continue to keep this silent also. We only wish it could be otherwise.''

"The truth will be out soon enough,'' James said.

"Before winter?'' Ed asked. "You're sure of that?''

"As soon as possible. Certainly before spring. And who knows, perhaps it will end quickly. That all depends on whether everyone cooperates.'' Dex grinned. "And on how quickly Reggoner and Mullen rise to the bait.''

"All right. We won't quarrel. But we hope . . .''

"So do we,'' Dex said. "So do we.''

Jasmine brightened. "Won't you come in for a snack? I have pie fresh out of the oven. And buttermilk. You like buttermilk don't you, James? Dexter said that you do.''

Early on Tuesday morning Dex was outside Benson's largest mercantile when the proprietor unlocked the door and opened for business.

"Are you the telegrapher, sir?'' Dex asked.

The storekeeper yawned. "No, that's my son. He's upstairs finishing his breakfast.''

"I need to send a wire.''

"Is it urgent?''

"It is . . . shall we say . . . important.'' Dex smiled. "But I'm sure the boy's mother would agree with me that another five minutes will make no difference. A young man needs to start his day properly.''

"Come inside then. Tell you what. You go ahead and write out your message. There's a counter over there by the postal window. Use the yellow pad for the telegram message. I'll go tell my son that you're waiting.''

"Tell him he needn't hurry unduly. This will take me some time, sir.''

Dex removed a slip of paper from his pocket and consulted it often as he wrote down the message he wished to send.

PRESIDENT, BATON ROUGE, HOUSTON AND PACIFIC
R.R., SQUIRES BLDG, BATON ROUGE.
KYPLH JNHRY WFRYH SIOLF QPDHN MDRUS AXOIZ
LPOFD 26 NOVEMBER LATEST GRUTL PCVBY WDEFL
STOP
SIGNED D Y

He formed his letters with care, then folded the sheet he'd been reading from—it was his laundry list from the previous week actually—and returned it to his pocket just as the storekeeper and a pasty-faced young man with lank hair and pimples returned to the store.

The boy looked at the message form, blinked and stared at Dex. "This is your message, Mr. Yancey?''

Dex found it interesting, and rather agreeable, that the youngster was aware of who he was. Good. That meant the boy was inclined to gossip. "Yes," he responded. "And please take care to copy it exactly. Accuracy is much more important to me than speed of transmission.''

"Yes, sir. I'll be real careful.''

Dex smiled, paid for the telegram and left.

On Wednesday afternoon Dex and James returned from their travels up and down the river early.

Dex wanted ample time to bathe and prepare himself for the evening.

He had, after all, made certain promises to Helena.

· 43 ·

Dex shuddered. The intensity of his climax was so strong that he literally cried out loud. Helena, sweet girl, was damned good when she set her mind—and certain other parts—to it.

She clung to him fiercely with arms, legs and teeth as if trying to draw him even deeper into herself and keep him there. Or, more to the point of the moment, trying to keep his semen there.

Dex moved just a little and she stopped biting his shoulder to whisper, "Don't take it out, honey. Not yet, please. It feels so nice there."

"I'm getting a cramp," he told her. "I have to get off you or else put all my weight on you."

"Stay, please," she said again. "You won't hurt me." She seemed pleased when he let his full weight down onto her slim body. And in truth she did not seem to be hurt in the least.

Dex kissed her and asked, "So. Do you feel pregnant now?"

Helena's eyes went wide and her pretty face took on a sudden look of concern. "Am I s'posed to already?"

Dex laughed and kissed the tip of her nose then each eye

before he answered. "No, dear. I was just teasing. That is, I never heard anyone say a girl is supposed to know right away. Not that I have any personal experience. I've never been a father."

"You won't be now either, honey. I meant it when I promised you that. Not like having to pay to raise the kid or nothing like that, I mean. All I want from you is this right here. I'll take care o' the rest of it. You won't ever even know if I'm knocked up. Okay?"

"Fine," he agreed. "As for whether you are or not, what I'm hoping for is that you will be happy, however this motherhood impulse turns out."

"I'll be a whole lot happier if I have a baby," Helena said.

"I do think you will make a fine mother," Dex told her. "Now or whenever it happens. And before I go, little dear, I'll see that you aren't without resources. Not a lot, perhaps, but I'll leave a little something with you."

"All I need you t' leave with me, Dexter honey, is that baby, an' maybe you done that already." She smiled up at him. "Though I reckon we should keep on tryin', just to kinda make sure, don't you think?"

"I concur," Dex said.

"Concur. That means, like, you agree?"

He nodded.

Helena sighed and kissed the side of his neck. "You can get off now, honey. But careful. Don't roll me around. I got to lay on my back here an' put some pillows under my butt for a spell."

"What's that for?"

"It's to keep your juice in a puddle way inside my pussy. That gives me the best chance for being knocked up."

"I never heard that before," he said as he carefully lifted himself from her and lay down at her side. Helena immediately reached for both pillows, her own and his too, wadded them as thick as she could manage and used them to elevate her hips.

"I never done it myself, o' course," she said. "Always before now wanted just the opposite to being preggers. But all the girls that work in the life know little tricks to keep from bein' pregnant an' other ones to help get that way.''

"In 'the life', did you say?"

"Yeah. You know. Whoring.'' Helena smiled. "The sportin' life, that's what we call it.''

"Oh, I see.''

"Some of it's bad. Some of it ain't so.''

"Will you stay in the business after you have your baby?'' he asked.

"Yeah, for a while, I guess.'' Then she laughed and added, "But if things keep up like they been lately I'll be able to afford something different. Leave this crappy little town and go someplace. New Orleans, maybe. Baton Rouge. Houston. I could go to one of them places and buy me a little store. Sell ladies duds or like that. I can afford it if Mr. Mullen keeps bribing me like he done so far.''

"Is it going well?'' Dex asked even though he was fairly sure he already knew the answer due to the fact that Mullen and Reggoner wanted to mend their fences with him.

"It's going along just like you said you want it to is what I'd say,'' Helena told him. "I added a little notion of my own though. I wouldn't tell him the whole story about you until he paid me. An' then I held back a few details so's he'd pay me some more.''

Dex laughed. "A very nice touch, my dear. I salute your perspicacity.''

"My what?''

"Never mind. Tell me everything that happened.''

"Sure. I went over to his house when I knew his missus wasn't around. She spends a lot o' time with her friends, playing cards or whatever. Mister George, he spends a lot o' evenings by himself.''

"However would you know that sort of thing?'' Dex asked.

Helena gave him a look that said he should know better. "Us sporting girls may not be high society, Dexter, but we pay attention to them that is. We like t' see what they wear an' how they act.'' She shrugged. "Part of it is jealousy, I guess, but some of it too is trying to figure out how come their husbands marry high but come see us when it's a healthy fuck or a blowjob they want. Anyway, it's true. We pay a lot of attention to the classy ladies.''

"Like Amanda Mullen," Dex suggested.

"Yeah, if you wanta call her classy."

"You wouldn't?"

"I don't want to talk about her, okay? Let me tell you how it went when I went to call on Mister George." She laughed. "Oh Dexter honey, it was fine. It really was. Like you said I could expect, except even better."

"You told him everything I wanted you to?"

Helena giggled. "Eventually. After he paid me enough."

"Good girl," Dex said. "Now try to remember everything you told him and everything Mullen said, everything he asked. Do you think you can do that?"

She gave him a coquettish look over her bare shoulder. "With Mister George I held out for more money. But with you, honey, it's another roll in the feathers that I'm demanding."

"Insatiable little wench, aren't you?"

"Uh huh. I surely am. An' I won't tell you nary thing more, honey, till you promise me another squirt of baby-making juice up the old twat."

"You know I'd give you that anyway."

"I want you to promise."

"All right. You win. I promise."

"Good," she squealed and started to roll onto her side to give him a hug, then remembered that she was supposed to be lying supine while she waited for his sperm to swim onto a waiting and receptive egg. "Oops," she yelped and flopped onto her back again before any damage could be done. "You'll have to come over here an' give me a hug, honey. Then I'll tell you every last little thing I can remember about me and Mister George. And *then*, honey, you and me will make the critter with two backs. How does that sounds?"

Dex kissed her and gave her the requested squeeze as

well. "I couldn't have planned it better myself, dear." He lay back on the bed, mildly regretful that Helena had swiped his pillow but not wanting to snatch it back now, and waited for the girl to tell her tale.

· 44 ·

"She didn't!" James exclaimed.

"She did," Dex insisted. "She told me so."

"Clever girl."

"And getting richer all the time," Dex agreed. He was in the hotel room, alone with James, going over with him all the things Helena had related about her visits with George Mullen.

Dex was feeling good. He had a fine breakfast under his belt and a good night behind him. Not a good night's sleep necessarily, but a very good night nonetheless.

"When will she talk to him again?"

Dex grinned. "She should be seeing him right about now."

"You went over with her what to say this time, I assume?"

"Of course. And it isn't any secret in town, I'm sure, that I spent the night with her. We might as well capitalize on that, so I told her to sneak right over there this morning. She'll go to the bank, like she wants to discuss an account or something, and see him in private there."

"Perfect," James said.

"She told me she'll volunteer just enough to get his interest up. Tell him that she led me into discussing land prices with her last night, but if he wants to know what I said then he'll have to come up with some cash to ease the knots out of her tongue.''

"She'll have enough put away to buy that shop in Houston before we're done here," James said.

"I hope she does."

"So what did you tell her to say about the land?''

"We know bottom land here is selling for five dollars tops, sometimes four or four-fifty the acre if a man wants a quick sale. So I told her to carry to Mullen the news that we will offer six dollars for all we can buy but that we can be talked into eight or, if push comes to shove we'd go as high as ten dollars an acre.''

James laughed. "Which means Mullen and your boy Charles will think they can push us as high as twelve dollars.''

"I certainly hope so," Dex said gleefully.

"You know," James mused, "I really do think you missed your calling in life. You really would make an awfully good thief.''

Dex laughed. "It isn't too late. And think about it. We have to find *some* way to make a living now that we don't have poor old Saladin to count on.''

"Yeah, but . . .''

Dex shrugged.

"So what do we do now? Sit and wait for your girlfriend's information to ferment?''

"Actually, I was doing some thinking last night.''

"Thinking, was it?''

"I didn't say I was *only* thinking. But a fellow has to do something while he's resting up and getting ready for seconds. Or thirds. Or whatever.''

"You know," James said in a serious tone, "I'd always heard that you white boys slow down after the first half dozen times or so. Always thought that was just an ugly rumor though. Now I find that it's true. Thank goodness I wasn't born with a handicap like that.''

"Are you paying attention? D'you want to hear my idea or don't you?"

"Yezzum, bawss, I's sorry."

Dex shook his head, then went on. "What I was thinking, James, is that you need to take a nice long ride today."

"Another ride? Jeez, Dex, I've been in the damn saddle every day for the past week or more. I'm starting to get saddle sores on top of my calluses from it all."

"Bear with me. I think you're going to like this."

Half an hour later James was in the saddle and riding at a jog toward the next town downriver.

• 45 •

Dex was lounging in the hotel lobby with a copy of the *New Orleans Picayune* open in his lap—only four days old too, not at all bad considering—when the boy from the mercantile found him.

"Mr. Yancey."

"Yes?"

"I have a telegram for you, sir." He scratched his head. "I hope I got it copied down all right. I had to go back and get the operator on the other end to repeat a couple times. I mean, regular messages, you kind of follow along and know what letter is coming next. This stuff, it's hard. But I did the best I could, sir."

"Thank you, son." Dex tipped the young man a quarter, a munificent amount really, and slightly inappropriate considering that he was not a message runner but the telegraph operator. The gesture was, however, a calculated one. It would give the fellow another reason to talk about the strange telegram Mr. Yancey received.

Dex made something of a show of folding his newspaper and laying it aside, waiting until the boy left before opening the message envelope. He took one look inside, then grunted and hurried upstairs to the privacy of his room.

The paper, of course, conveyed nothing but gibberish. Random letters put together with no meaning save for the two plain language words inserted in the middle of the text, OCTOBER LATEST.

Dex smiled. It was good service, really. The telegram was already here and it was barely the middle of the afternoon.

He didn't expect James to return from sending it until nightfall or later.

· 46 ·

"I think," Dex said, "it's time we enter the third phase of this little scheme of ours."

"So quick?" James asked.

"Yeah, I think so. If we screw around too long we're apt to do something to mess it up. Besides, I'm not that crazy about this town. There's some bad memories here. I want to see some new country. Austin, San Antonio, maybe on out to New Mexico and Arizona next."

"It's all the same to me," James said. "Besides, I don't believe for a minute that you're worried about our plan. You just want an excuse to spend another night with that Helena girl."

"I will admit that there are worse things that could happen," Dex said with a grin. "But I do think we can move along now." He looked at the telegram message in his hand, the second he'd received in a week. It had only three groups of gobbledygook on it and made no sense at all. Except perhaps to George Mullen and Charles Reggoner, and they were welcome to interpret it however their imaginations provided.

He wondered if they'd thought about bribing or other-

wise acquiring information from the young telegrapher. He
certainly hoped they had.

"All right," James said. "Tomorrow I'll go visit with
Ed and Jasmine. Make sure they know what to say if one
of our boys comes along wanting to make an offer."

"Good enough. Before noon tomorrow," Dex said,
"Mullen will have been told that the railroad is ready to
start acquiring options on a right of way with the offers
starting at six dollars per acre."

James smiled. "You figure Reggoner will counter at
seven?"

"Better yet at eight. He'll want to strike quick and get
his options on paper all signed, sealed and recorded before
we get wind of what he's doing. After all, he can't outgun
a railroad in a bidding war, and there wouldn't be any point
to it if he could. The whole idea is to set him up so he
thinks he can make a profit by buying the land at something
considerably less than he knows. . . . or believes he knows
. . . we will go, then selling his options to the railroad at a
handsome profit."

"We'll know how well this thing is likely to work as
soon as Helena sells her new information to Mullen,"
James said.

"I'll have her tell him tomorrow that I intend offering
options late this week, starting with Ed Bryant."

"What do you bet Reggoner shows up at their farm before dark tomorrow night."

"I damn sure hope he does. Just don't let him see you
out there without me. That would tip him that something
isn't right."

"Don't worry. I'll visit with them early and be gone
from there long before Reggoner could get the word and
ride out to them."

"And as quick as he strikes his deal, tell Ed to spread
the word all up and down the river. Price, terms, the whole
thing."

James laughed. "There's an awful lot of people who are
gonna end up owing us for helping them out of a jam that
they don't even know they're in."

"Won't know we got them out of it either if we're lucky," Dex said. "They're welcome to their profit. It doesn't take anything away from us."

"You think we'll make out on the deal too?"

"If I have our boy George figured out properly, we will. With Helena's help."

"You trust her to plant that seed for us?"

"Uh huh. She's a smart girl." Dex grinned. "I wouldn't be surprised if she brings it off so slick that old George will wind up thinking it was his idea to begin with.

"Well I don't know about you, but I'm getting hungry. I'm going to go down for supper, then head over to the saloon to find Helena."

"Hungry hell," James said. "You're horny, that's all."

Dex looked positively wounded by the accusation. "I'm hungry," he insisted. Then added, "*And* horny."

"Don't expect me to wait up for you."

"Good, because you'd have one hell of a long night if you did." Dex stood, stretched, then reached for his coat, hat and cane.

He was looking forward to another evening with Helena.

· 47 ·

Dex accepted a glass of buttermilk—James wasn't having any—from Jasmine Bryant and leaned back in great satisfaction. "It worked," he said.

"Like a charm," Ed Bryant agreed.

"May we see?"

Bryant nodded, and Jasmine once more disappeared into their bedroom to fetch a document from the trunk that held their treasures. She brought it back and handed it to James, who opened it and laid it onto the kitchen table between them so he and Dex could both read it at once.

The paper in question was a binding contract, signed by both Charles Reggoner and Edwin Lee Bryant, giving Reggoner an option to purchase Bryant's farm on the banks of the Neches River. The purchase price, should the option be exercised, was set at $8.50 per acre.

Dex whistled when he saw that. "So much," he said.

Ed smiled and shrugged. "Jasmine thought it was worth a try. She was right."

"But he had to promise he wouldn't tell the neighbors what price was agreed to," Jasmine put in.

"Will you?" James asked.

"No, indeed," Bryant declared. "I gave the man my word."

"Fortunately for the neighbors," Jasmine said, "Mr. Reggoner never thought to ask for my silence. And there are more than a few Negro hired hands working on the farms up and down this river. I can safely tell the particulars to them, and they will pass the word along to their employers. Before the week is out everyone who needs to will know exactly the option price Ed got from him. And most especially they will know *all* the details."

"He paid you a fair price for the option?" Dex asked.

Both Ed and Jasmine grinned hugely. "Just like you suggested," Ed said. "First and foremost we insisted on him forgiving the equipment loan from last spring . . . which he did on the spot, signed it off as being satisfied and we have that document put away with his signature on it in good, dark ink . . . plus he gave us some cash up front to bind the option with. Normal would have been for him to bind the option with ten percent, but because he was writing off the equipment loan too we agreed to accept only five percent of the end price in exchange for giving him the option."

"Which won't ever be exercised, of course," Dex said. "Once we've slipped off into the sunset and they know there is no railroad being planned to Caddo Lake, Reggoner and Mullen couldn't possibly exercise those options. They'd be buying at eight-fifty only to find themselves stuck with farm land worth five dollars. And they'd likely have to take less than that once word got around that there was a glut of good bottom land on the Benson real estate market. It could drop as low as four dollars, I'd think."

"The option payment is found money for us," Jasmine said, "and we thank you for it. Not only do we have the equipment free and clear, now we have cash in hand too. Ed and I have talked this over, and I think we should share it with you. You're entitled to half." She reached into an apron pocket and withdrew a lump of folded currency that she handed to James.

Or tried to. He refused to accept the money.

"Don't worry about us, lady. We are gonna make out just fine by ourselves," James told her.

"It doesn't hardly seem right," Jasmine said.

"Taking the money from Reggoner and Mullen, you mean?"

"Lord, no. They tried to steal our land from us. Getting back at them is only fair. What I meant was you two gentlemen arranging all this so that we benefit and not getting anything out of it for yourselves."

"Oh, we intend to come out healthy," Dex told her.

"I don't understand."

Dex only grinned and said, "Greedy men tend to see greed in everyone else too, even where there isn't any. We expect to put that trait to work for us." He paused and then added, "Could I ask one favor though, Mrs. Bryant?" He knew good and well that it pleased Jasmine to hear anyone call her that and especially so to hear it from a white man.

"You know you can ask me most anything, Mr. Yancey."

"In that case, ma'am, I'd surely like another glass of that fine buttermilk from your churning."

She hurried away from the table to get it. And did not bother to ask James if he wanted any. By now she knew better.

· 48 ·

Dex struggled with his boot, then with a grunt of effort managed to pull it on. He stood, stomped both feet to make sure everything was as it should be and turned to inspect himself in the mirror before fetching his coat and cane.

"Off to see your lady again," James observed.

"Time to drive the last nail into their coffin, I think," Dex said.

"By way of Helena, I presume."

Dexter nodded. "She has George Mullen convinced that my bedroom talk is boasting and braggadocio." He grinned. "Handy, that is."

"Yes, and this one is for us. The rubes who live around here are being taken care of—by the way, did I mention to you that that white ofay son of a bitch Reggoner has been spending his days riding from farm to farm lately—but this time the benefit will be ours."

Dex squinted into the mirror and tugged first one loop of his tie, then the other. Darn thing looked lopsided no matter which way he pulled it. "Dammit! Would you get off your butt and help me with this thing, please."

James stood, yawned and shuffled across the room to

give the tie one quick tweak, then with a grunt went back to the cot where he'd been stretched out.

"That's all?" Dex asked.

"It's a question of knowing what you're doing. Which you don't, white boy."

Dex inspected the result in the mirror. It would have pleased him to be able to tell James that the tie was still awry. Unfortunately, the damn thing was perfect now. "How do you know where Charles has been?" he asked without turning away from the mirror.

"Us shadow folk aren't just in the towns, you know. I let a few people know I was interested, and the whispers have been going up and down the river. Do you want a list of which exact farms he's already done business with? Give me a couple days and I could get one."

"No, but it wouldn't hurt for us to know how much longer he needs to wrap up his options." Dex laughed. "I can't wait to see their faces when they find out the tables are turned on them and that they're the ones who are out, not us."

"Personally I'd rather be somewhere else when they learn it," James said. "Where was it you said you wanted to go next? Austin? That would be just about far enough away for when they learn the truth."

"Not me," Dex told him. "I want to be there. I want to see it in their eyes when the light breaks over the horizon."

"Metaphorically speaking, I hope. You know I don't like having to get up early."

Dex gave him a dirty look.

"I'll ask some questions tonight," James said. "See if we can figure out how much more time we need to make sure all the farmers have their option money in hand and their equipment debts canceled."

"Everyone is expecting the same deal? Cancel the original notes and accept five percent against the option?"

James nodded. Then laughed. "Everybody except one sorry old son of a bitch who's holding out for cancellation of the debt and fifteen percent. But don't worry about him. He's a skinflint and a slapper."

"A slapper?"

"Likes to slap his workers around. Pays them pennies, feeds them crap and likes to hit them if they're working too slow to suit him. He might end up being stung in spite of all this, and if he does, well, fuck 'im. He deserves it."

"Is that a touch of mean-spiritedness I hear, James?"

"I like the girl who does his housework. It isn't pretty the way he treats her. She deserves better. Hell, a dog deserves better."

"In that case I expect I won't worry about him either. If he's too thick to agree to a good thing there's nothing you or I can do for him."

"Like I said. Serves the son of a bitch right. You know what to tell Helena tonight, right?"

"Just like we talked about," Dex said. He picked up his hat and spent a few extra seconds adjusting it to an angle that pleased him, then touched the head of his cane to the hat brim by way of a salute.

"Don't wait up for me," he said as he headed for the door.

◆ 49 ◆

"Mr. Yancey."

"Yes, Mr. Mullen?"

"I was hoping I might be fortunate enough to run into you today. Would you care to join me, sir?"

Hoping. Sure, Dex thought. He took practically every meal in this same hotel dining room, morning, noon and night, and now Mullen expressed surprise to see him here? Yeah, that was certainly believable. You bet it was. "It would be my pleasure, sir."

Dexter accepted a chair at Mullen's table. They exchanged remarks about the weather. Ordered lunch. Laughed at a few jokes. The pork chops and fried potatoes hadn't yet been served though when Mullen broached the subject that brought him here.

"May I discuss something with you, Mr. Yancey? Something that is, shall we say, of a delicate nature?"

"Of course, Mr. Mullen. Anything you wish."

"Yes, well, I do not in any way intend to offend you, sir, nor to imply anything untoward. But . . . frankly, Mr. Yancey, it has come to my attention that you may not be, um, how shall I put this . . . ?"

"Be direct if you please, Mr. Mullen. I've already given

you leave to speak plainly. I assure you I'll not be offended.''

"Yes, um . . . I have reason to believe that you are at the moment not on the best of terms with your employer?''

"I think I shall offer no comment on that, sir.''

"I believe you find yourself in need of funds and that they are refusing to grant an advance on your wages?''

Dex drew back rather stiffly. But he did not deny the claim. "Go on, sir.''

"Truly, Mr. Yancey, my intention has not been to pry. This knowledge came to me by way of a friend in the Baton Rouge offices of the railroad. He mentioned it only because he knew you are in Benson, you see, and wondered if we might be acquainted.''

Dex kept both his expression and his spine rigid. He also marveled at the coincidences involved. Especially so in that he himself had invented both the railroad and its Baton Rouge address. How very odd that George Mullen would know someone who worked there. "Go on, sir.''

"As you know, Mr. Yancey, you are a great favorite of my partner. He likes you very much. As I do myself. And I feel a certain, well, obligation, one might say. Because of the unforgivable behavior of my brother-in-law Charles shortly after you arrived.''

"That is water beneath the bridge at this point, I assure you.''

"I am glad to hear you say that, Mr. Yancey, but I feel a certain responsibility regardless. A family thing, you might say.''

"I can understand how that could be, sir,'' Dex agreed.

"It would please me, Mr. Yancey, if you would permit Charles and me to make amends.''

"I take it that you have some means in mind?'' Dex said.

"Yes, we, uh, we thought perhaps you might enjoy a vacation. I know you've been working long and diligently on behalf of your employers.'' Dex had been lying about in the sunshine—figuratively speaking, that is—practically from the moment they arrived in Benson. Overwork was hardly a problem for him or for James either one. But then nearly everyone views himself as put-upon. Men like George Mullen and Charles Reggoner counted on that trait when they endeavored to cheat and steal from their fellows.

"I *have* been feeling rather tired of late," Dex said.

"Perhaps you would allow Charles and me to provide you with funds for a relaxing trip. To Galveston, perhaps? I know you enjoy gambling. And, if I may mention it, the ladies. Galveston offers exceptional opportunity in both those areas of interest."

"I've never been to Galveston," Dex mused. "But I've heard it is quite expensive." He gave Mullen a sly smile. "Something else I've heard is that you and Charles have been buying up options on certain acreages in this vicinity. Do you intend to go into large-scale farming, George? Or will I find myself negotiating with you at the end of my vacation?" The smile broadened. "If I, too, may be blunt, sir."

Mullen chuckled. "I appreciate honesty, Mr. Yancey, I surely do. How much do you think it would require for you to take a two-week vacation?"

"Oh, perhaps another five hundred, sir."

"Five hundred is a great deal of money, Mr. Yancey."

"Five hundred is the same amount your brother-in-law acted so disagreeably about," Dex reminded him. "And if I may be so bold as to mention it, five hundred is a pittance when considered against the amount of profit you intend me to help you take from the railroad."

"You did say you intended honesty in this discussion, didn't you?" Mullen said.

"Five hundred is what I think would be fair," Dex said. "By the bye, did your friend in Baton Rouge mention to you that I have the authority to change the specifics of the route if I wish? I could take it up the other bank of the Neches if I want. I daresay the officers of the road would thank me if I could show them a savings in land prices large enough to justify the expense of another bridge or two." His smile was smarmy and smug. Or anyway he did his best to make it such.

Mullen frowned. Then, accepting the inevitable, he nodded. "Five hundred."

"In cash, if you please."

"I will have it ready for you first thing tomorrow morning. You may call at the bank, as before."

"And I will make immediate plans for a short vacation," Dex responded.

"All right. I believe we understand each other."

"Yes, perhaps we do." Better, Dex thought, than George Mullen yet knew.

Mullen laid his napkin beside his plate and stood.

"You aren't waiting for your dinner, sir?"

"There are business affairs that I only now remember. If you will excuse me, sir?"

"Yes, of course." Dex stood and shook the man's hand—he could always wash afterward—and added, "Give my regards to Charles, if you please."

"Certainly." Mullen nodded, rather stiffly he thought, and left the hotel.

Dex remained and enjoyed a most satisfying meal. Dear, dear Helena, he was thinking. He really did think they should grant her a bonus for her efforts. The girl was quite a help.

· 50 ·

Dex and James rode into Benson from the south. They stopped first to allow the horses to drink from the public water trough, then walked them the final block to the bank building.

"Is Mr. Mullen here?" Dex asked the clerk.

"No, sir, I believe he is at Mr. Reggoner's office at the moment. He said something about having business there."

"And that would be . . . ?"

The man gave directions. It wasn't far. But then it could not have been. Benson was not big enough for anything to be too far.

Dex found the address easily. Gilt lettering on the second-floor door read C.B. REGGONER, ATTY AT LAW. Dex turned the knob and entered without knocking. It was, after all, a business office.

Reggoner was seated at an impressively weighty rolltop desk while George Mullen was lounging in an upholstered armchair. There were a silver serving pot and an assortment of crullers on a small table between them.

"Good morning," Dex said. James stood silent behind him.

"You're back early," Reggoner said. "You were supposed to be gone for two weeks. This is only one. I'm warning you, if you came back thinking you could extort more money from us . . ."

"Not at all," Dex said with a bright and charming smile. "That is the furthest thing from my mind, I promise you."

"What is it then?" Mullen asked. He too made no pretense toward friendliness now. But then after all, he and Charles already established that Dexter Yancey could be bribed and was unworthy of high social standing. Hadn't they?

Dex's smile did not waver. "It's safe enough to return now," he said. "You have all your options in place. You signed the final one last night. Gave a man named Ormand eighty-five dollars and satisfaction of the note you held against his farm."

"How the devil would you know a thing like that?" Mullen demanded.

"Maybe I didn't go quite as far away as Galveston," Dex said. "And maybe I've been paying attention."

"Do you want to negotiate a price for the railroad now? Is that it? You want to offer to exchange a higher cost to your employers for another cash payment direct into your own pocket? Is that it? Well, name your terms then. But you should be aware that I already know you can go as high as twelve dollars an acre and no higher. So you haven't as much to bargain with as you think." Mullen looked quite satisfied with himself. "Knowledge is power, Mr. Yancey. It is a lesson you will soon understand."

Dex laughed. "I agree, Mr. Mullen. Accurate knowledge can be vital. But please note that I did say 'accurate.' "

"What is that supposed to mean?" Reggoner demanded, his tone peevish. Dex suspected it still rankled him that he'd been forced to pay the five-hundred-dollar gaming debt when Saladin beat Reggoner's nag.

"It means that you two don't know quite as much as you think you do. Did your friend in Baton Rouge tip you about the price limits, George?"

"What if he did?" Mullen shot back.

"I find it fascinating, that's all. All the more so because

there is no railroad. The road doesn't exist, and there is no
Baton Rouge office.''

"The hell you say!''

"You got your information from that empty-headed little
whore. I've been deliberately telling her things, hoping that
the cheap little slut would run and tell someone about it. I
see that she did.'' Dex hated talking about Helena that way.
She was a sweet girl, never mind what she did for a living.
But she lived here. And he did not want Mullen and Reggoner taking their wrath out on her when Dex and James
were gone.

"You've been gulled, boys. Led around like a pair of
immature oxen with rings in your noses and blinders pulled
snug over your eyes. You got so greedy trying to steal from
your neighbors that you never stopped to think that it might
have been you who was being set up. So go ahead and
exercise your options if you like. Then see if you can sell
that land to somebody for anything close to what you paid
for it. Or just swallow your losses and think hard the next
time you want to steal from somebody. Because I—or
somebody like me—just might be waiting around ready to
turn the tables on you, you low, miserable excuses for hu-
manity. Neither one of you is man enough to wipe a real
gentleman's ass.'' Dex tipped his hat in their direction.
"Good day to you. And fuck you both.''

He turned and left the law office with James on his heels.

"Dammit, Dex, I still think we should've let them learn
about this slow. And with us a week's ride away from
here.''

"Naw, it was worth it. Did you see the look on Charles's
face? He looked like he'd been hit over the head with a
maul. And George didn't look much happier. I say it
couldn't have worked out any nicer. Why . . .''

His soliloquy was interrupted by the slam of a door
above just as Dex reached street level from the flight of
stairs leading up to Reggoner's office.

He heard the door slam and immediately afterward the

soft but rather nastily distinctive click of a revolver action being cocked.

It occurred to him even as he was turning to look that the pleasant liveryman Henry Adams did once mention something about Charles being quick on the shoot.

· 51 ·

"Whoa, now. Hold on there. No need to get excited and do something you'll regret later," Dex said, peering up the stairs at Charles Reggoner who stood there with a very large and ugly revolver in his hand.

"I won't regret any of it, believe me," Reggoner said.

Dex was beginning to feel more than a trifle naked. Safety was several paces distant. And Adams had said that Charles was quick. And accurate, too. The combination seemed particularly unpleasant right now.

"I tell you what. I'll give your money back. Not just the five hundred. All of it. A thousand dollars. What you paid me and what I won, too. That should help ease the pain, shouldn't it?"

He smiled and transferred his cane to his left hand. Damn sword isn't worth much when the adversary is twenty feet away and has a gun in his hand, he was discovering. "I have it right here."

Reggoner held his fire while Dex reached inside his coat.

Dex was still smiling when he brought his hand out again.

But instead of a wad of money, which James carried

anyway, he had a pipsqueak little .32 revolver in hand.

Reggoner blinked, perhaps unsure of what he was seeing. Or perhaps unable to take seriously the threat of such a tiny pistol.

The man looked quite on the verge of laughter.

Until Dex's wee gun barked, the sound of its report hardly louder than that of a tree limb snapping, and a moist red dimple appeared just above the bridge of Charles Reggoner's nose.

Dexter was not particularly fast with a pistol, but he was hell for accurate.

Reggoner's head jerked back and a look of sheer amazement came over him. Then his knees buckled, and he tumbled head-first down the stairs to land in an untidy sprawl in the dirt.

James had to step quickly sideways to avoid being run into by the falling body. Dex noted that James somehow had come up with a flat rock that he was clutching.

"Going to brain him, were you? You David, he Goliath?"

"What, are you complaining?"

"Not me, no indeed."

"It was all I could think of," James explained. "Either that or run up the stairs and bite him on the ankle. I hope you'll forgive me for rejecting that option."

"Remind me to buy you a gun," Dex said. "Black man or not, it wouldn't do any hurt for you to have a gun handy. Out of sight but handy."

"Does that mean you're planning to do more stuff like this?"

Dex gave his friend an innocent look. And then had to pay attention to the others as George Mullen came storming down the stairs demanding Dexter's arrest—actually he seemed to have something on the order of a hanging in mind, but custom even in Texas would demand an arrest and trial beforehand—while two women who'd been standing on the sidewalk nearby were exclaiming just as forcefully that Charles Reggoner attacked poor Mr. Yancey without provocation.

Dex decided to remain silent on the subject of who provoked whom and let the ladies defend him however they pleased.

· 52 ·

"Mmm, nice. Very nice. Yes, dear. There. Like that is good, yes. Oooh. Deep and slow. I like that."

He did, too. There was something about having his cock warm and wet inside a pretty woman's mouth that pleased him all out of proportion to the sensations that were involved.

Maybe it had to do with being able to lie there and watch. Quite apart from the exquisite feel of it all, he just loved to see a woman's cheeks hollow as she sucked and suckled and pulled him in.

And this, this was as nice as he could remember it being. This girl was *good*.

"You like it?" she asked, withdrawing from him only by fractions of an inch. He could still feel her breath light and cool as it wafted over flesh made slippery with her saliva.

"No, I don't just like it. I love it. I dote on it. I adore the way you suck a cock. If there's ever a statue erected to honor the giver of perfect blowjobs it will be your image they choose."

She smiled, obviously very happy with the flattery.

But then, Dex noted, there is no such thing

as a surfeit of flattery. Too much is usually barely enough, and this particular recommendation was no exception to that rule.

"A statue would be cold," she said.

"You aren't cold," he agreed.

"A statue would be hard."

"You, my dear, are soft as an angel's kiss. But you do make me hard, bless you."

She preened and giggled just a little.

"I didn't mean to disturb you," he said. "Feel free to go back to what you were doing."

"Do you want me to?"

"Mm, very much so."

"You like this?" she asked.

"Yes."

"And this?"

He groaned.

"What about this?"

Dex closed his eyes and shuddered. If it got any better he wouldn't be able to stand it. "Jeez," he exclaimed, opening his eyes again. Something else he couldn't stand was the idea of wasting a chance to watch such supreme talent in action.

Nobody, nowhere could play the skin flute like this girl could. Damn but she was fine.

She pulled away from him again. "I do love doing this, dear, and normally I would want to keep it up until you faint." Dex wasn't entirely sure she was kidding about that either. He thought it entirely possible that she could manage it. "But under the circumstances, sweetie, I think I should finish you off quickly this time." She smiled sweetly. "I don't want to deprive myself of the taste of your juice, you see, but I want to have this lovely thing inside me, too, so I think time is of the essence. After all, we only have so much time to enjoy ourselves before George gets back from the funeral."

"Of course, Amanda. Whatever you think best."

She buried her pretty face in his crotch again, hard this

time so that all he could see on the downstrokes was a mass of sleek red hair in his lap.

Dex sighed. This was small of him, he was sure. Petty. And Mullen would never even know he'd been cuckolded, the dumb sonuvabitch.

But Dex did not regret doing it. Not for a second, he didn't.

"There," he said. "Yes. Fast now. Ahhhhh!"

JAKE LOGAN
TODAY'S HOTTEST ACTION WESTERN!

**Explore the exciting Old West with one
of the men who made it wild!**